NEW YORK REVIEW
CLASSICS

MRS PALFREY AT THE CLAREMONT

ELIZABETH TAYLOR (1912–1975) was born into a middle-class family in Berkshire, England. She held a variety of positions, including librarian and governess, before marrying a businessman in 1936. Nine years later, her first novel, *At Mrs. Lippincote's*, appeared. She would go on to publish eleven more novels (including *Angel* and *A Game of Hide and Seek*), four collections of short stories (many of which originally appeared in *The New Yorker*, *Harper's*, and other magazines), and a children's book, *Mossy Trotter*, while living with her husband and two children in Buckinghamshire. Long championed by Ivy Compton-Burnett, Barbara Pym, Robert Liddell, Kingsley Amis, and Elizabeth Jane Howard, Taylor's novels and stories have been the basis for a number of films, including *Mrs. Palfrey at the Claremont*, starring Joan Plowright, and François Ozon's *Angel*.

MICHAEL HOFMANN is a German-born, British-educated poet, critic, and translator. His most recent books are *One Lark, One Horse* (poems) and *Messing About in Boats* (essays). For New York Review Books he has translated several works, including Alfred Döblin's *Berlin Alexanderplatz*, and edited an anthology of writing by Malcolm Lowry, *The Voyage That Never Ends*.

OTHER BOOKS BY ELIZABETH TAYLOR
PUBLISHED BY NYRB CLASSICS

Angel
Introduction by Hilary Mantel

A Game of Hide and Seek
Introduction by Caleb Crain

A View of the Harbour
Introduction by Roxana Robinson

*You'll Enjoy It When You Get There: The Stories of
Elizabeth Taylor*
Selected and with an introduction by Margaret Drabble

MRS PALFREY AT THE CLAREMONT

ELIZABETH TAYLOR

Introduction by
MICHAEL HOFMANN

NEW YORK REVIEW BOOKS

New York

THIS IS A NEW YORK REVIEW BOOK
PUBLISHED BY THE NEW YORK REVIEW OF BOOKS
435 Hudson Street, New York, NY 10014
www.nyrb.com

First published as an NYRB Classic in 2021.

Library of Congress Cataloging-in-Publication Data
Names: Taylor, Elizabeth, 1912–1975, author. | Hofmann, Michael,
 1957 August 25– writer of introduction.
Title: Mrs. Palfrey at the Claremont / by Elizabeth Taylor ; introduction by
 Michael Hofmann.
Description: New York : New York Review Books, [2021] | Series: New York
 Review Books classics
Identifiers: LCCN 2021021170 (print) | LCCN 2021021171 (ebook)
 | ISBN 9781681375649 (paperback) | ISBN 9781681375656 (ebook)
Subjects: LCGFT: Novels.
Classification: LCC PR6039.A928 M5 2021 (print) | LCC PR6039.A928
 (ebook) | DDC 823/.914—dc23
LC record available at https://lccn.loc.gov/2021021170
LC ebook record available at https://lccn.loc.gov/2021021171

ISBN 978-1-68137-564-9
Available as an electronic book; ISBN 978-1-68137-565-6

Printed in the United States of America on acid-free paper.
10 9 8 7 6 5 4 3 2

INTRODUCTION

MRS PALFREY *at the Claremont* was first published in 1971, the eleventh of twelve novels by the English novelist Elizabeth Taylor. It has claims—I don't know the numbers—to being her most popular book. It takes its place in Robert McCrum's 2015 *Guardian* list of the one hundred best novels in English. On its first appearance, it was short-listed for the Booker Prize, then in its third year. Students of the prize will tell you that a good big one—or sometimes only a moderately good big one—will usually defeat a good—or even a very good—little one, and that's what happened this time too. The prize duly went to V. S. Naipaul's (I think rather messy book) *In a Free State*. The story goes that a jet-lagged Saul Bellow, acting as celebrity judge, thought he heard a lot of tinkling teacups in *Mrs Palfrey*, and there went her chances. By my reckoning, just one cup of tea is drunk in the entire novel—the one in Ludo's basement pad—and that doesn't tinkle. There are a handful of other references to tea, as it were unconsummated, and all of them non-tinkling. Bellow's crude point would have been better made by complaining about the presence in the book of pounds and pence, or the references to medium sherry. But sometimes Anglophobia, or perhaps the unbearable imputation of gentility, only has to harrumph to get its way.

Kingsley Amis described *Mrs Palfrey* in his *New Statesman* review as a novel about "loneliness, old age and approaching death." In terms of brute fact, his message is about the same as that of a standard contemporary reader's review, which sees a "detailed description of old people, slow, and a little depressing." That, though, comes with a steady subcutaneous drip—in "detailed," in "old," in "slow" and "little" and "depressing." Even "description" strikes me as disingenuous and wrong. One can hear in it the whine of mingled plaintiveness and balked self-adoration, the authentic who-needs-this huffing of our Tripadvisor-y times, the Age of Experian, or the New Irk. What we like is "relatable," whatever that means, while what we dislike or makes us uncomfortable is "depressing." What hope is there for our species if narcissism governs us even when we are *reading*? In *Angel*, her historical novel about a popular historical novelist, Taylor writes of her heroine's reading habits: "She had never cared much for books, because they did not seem to be about her." This surely is "relatability" in all its stupid glory, and fifty years before it was even invented. I find Amis's description to be true, candid, and economical. It even manages to sound a little zestful.

Mrs. Palfrey—Laura Palfrey—is a recently widowed grandmother. The Claremont is a residential hotel on Cromwell Road, the great traffic artery leading west out of London to Slough, Heathrow, and, ultimately, Bristol, on its way slicing through the tony borough of Kensington and Chelsea. ("I like the idea of Kensington Gore," Taylor has written elsewhere. Like all good novelists, she likes her names and place-names. They are free words, words she doesn't need to write. The biddable Mrs. Post. The bibulous, button-pressing Mrs. Burton. Ludo. Rosie. Old Bordon the boarding-school teacher. "Basil *whom*?" Coming from Taylor, even "old friends from Potters Bar" has an ominous ring: it is where people go to get potted.) Mrs. Palfrey has arrived at the Claremont by way of Rottingdean (another real place, near Brighton), and before that, Burma, where Mr. Palfrey—Arthur, her one-and-only, or once-and-future—will have been something in the colonial administration. (The British left there in 1948, just before Partition.) Burma (Myanmar) was known as the Scottish Colony, but only because of the preponderance in its government of men called Scott. Mrs. Palfrey's daughter, Elizabeth, has gone to live in Scotland, and has—troublingly even to Ian, her husband, let alone Mrs. Palfrey—become more Scottish than the Scots. ("She was not bred to Hogmanay, or dancing reels, or going out with the guns.") In Foreign Office parlance, she has "gone native." In its dry way, and while hardly an allegory, this novel about a handful of decayed gentlefolk, with its cast of female outlivers and one or two retired army officers, is a book about the state of postimperial England. Somewhere near the end, Taylor writes: "It was like watching a famous statue topple over. Prone, and broken, she was hardly Mrs Palfrey." The theme is the theme of England: the possibility of retreat, of a managed, or even dignified, withdrawal (because morning in England, to coin a fanciful expression, was in the seventeenth century). This is the seventh age. There is no reason why it shouldn't be of interest to us in our project—individually, nationally, collectively—of staying alive.

To Mrs. Palfrey, the old colonial hand, with her startling memories of teeming rain and snakes and restless natives, London is seen as a reasonable card to play, with the Natural History Museum within striking distance. (Not that she, or any of the other residents of the Claremont, ever goes there.)

It is 1968 or 1969 (Taylor quotes a couple of lines from "She's Leaving Home" from *Sgt. Pepper's*). Perhaps 1970, when the Queen Mum turned seventy. The world is suddenly getting younger. Men—including the dishy Ludo—have been growing their hair. Women, too. The typical three-story London terraced house is being broken up into flats, and prices are on their way through the roof. The Englishman's house is his...what, exactly? His investment—correct. From the basement—called the lower ground floor—one can see up from the bottom of what is aptly called a well about as far as the knees of passersby (it is Ludo's first vision of Laura; when he visits his mother's "frowsty little love-nest" in Putney, so much light and air make him giddy). People are always hungry, always thirsty, always starved of entertainment. Coffee is an unwise—and expensive—pretension, food has not yet been invented. Drink is sought after but, except on very special occasions, ditto. Ludo, one reads, "dived into a corner pub and bought two bottles of light ale, then hastened on to open and warm some spaghetti hoops. Rosie was coming to supper." Lucky girl. The young people flock like starlings to Trafalgar Square on Saturday nights, to get up to their bit of no good, I'm sure. There are nightly demonstrations on television—nuclear disarmament, maybe, or anti–Vietnam War, the elderly viewers would sooner not know. Accents—even the Queen's—are going to pot. Manners aren't what they used to be. The whole country seems to be in a bit of a pother, but, oddly, there are Union Jacks everywhere. Can it be that they no longer really signify anything beyond some get-rich-quick Carnaby Street wheeze? There is plenty for the reactionary-minded Osmonds of the world to react against, in the form of poison-pen letters to the papers, which themselves are spoiled for choice. The long-established post-WWII meanness of locked stationery drawers and no indoor heat and anxiety about sudden taxi fares and the price of stamps clashes with a strange newfangled sybaritism and cosmopolitanism in the young. Foreign travel is now a possibility. Weird restaurants are opened. "Crispy noodles I dote on," Rosie exclaims. "Oh, water chestnuts!" To some, as they used to say—as it might be, the eaters of the repeating cucumber sandwiches—nasty foreign muck. (This is decades before "Balti Britain." As I say, food hadn't really been invented.) Alert readers will pick up a steady stream of authentic fashion tips as well. You can build your very own Rita Tushingham from crushed velvet, "roll-ons" (British for "pantyhose"), PVC coats, white tights, white boots (these last, from memory, especially horrific). There is an unforgettable "description"—perhaps the only actual description in the book—of Rosie, styled almost like a Keatsian corpse: "Her long hair was straight, and dyed an old woman's grey. Her pale face was touching in its unhealthiness, the mournful eyes, the colourless lips. She was staring ahead of her." All the old ancestral values have been reevaluated: "Her parents would not have understood that, for the girl flat-dwellers, clothes came before food; fun before comfort; privacy nowhere. To him, the priorities were reversed, with privacy first, the assuagement of hunger next (which was different from having a meal), and clothes last." Among many other ways, one can read *Mrs Palfrey at the*

Claremont as an authoritative dissenting take on Swinging London. Swingeing London.

Taylor is a master of awkward, complicated, unexpected, and often unacknowledged feelings—it is what makes her such a consummate British artist. The Claremont is not so much full of old bones and replete with fragrant old memories as it is a hive of cruelty, dread, emulousness, arrogance, and humiliation. The phrase "exquisite torment" might have been especially invented for her. In the English way, she inflicts an exotic emotional education on the reader and calls it comedy. Words are either weapons or wounds. An unexpected kindness makes way in an instant for a devastating snub. As Taylor notes, the most outrageous sentiments can come in the wake of a seemingly guileless "I simply wondered..." or "I'm afraid..." It is as predictably unpredictable as the English weather. No, it *is* the English weather. "She suffered a little flurry of unpopularity when she asked for their coffee to be served at the table." One hears the hailstones pattering across her tablecloth. Elsewhere, it's cloudy with a chance of meatballs. "She saw a look of uncertainty on his face, and glanced quickly aside." "She looked at him with astonishment—her first change of expression from disdain." "He looked quite astounded at the idea—really appalled; and then the look of glee came back into his eyes." Was something said a moment ago pleasant or foul? Ought I to feel flattered or dismayed? Is something a rote phrase or does it actually mean something? There are moments of subtle slippage, when one observation is shared between two objects, or possibly neither: "'So nice,' she murmured, meaning the party, not the peanut." The insufferable Osmond roars out his obscenities; later, one feels sorry for him. Is he queer, frustrated, or just infantile? "'What is plonk?' Mrs Post asked nervously one morning." By evening, having found out, she is airing her "new trilling voice." "Mrs Arbuthnot, on one of her worst arthritis days, condoled with her spitefully." The combination here of verb and adverb is one of genius. Simpler natures will struggle with it. No wonder Mrs. Palfrey is unable to sleep after being its object. Taylor takes great pains to present her heroine as someone who can take care of herself: mannish, well-accoutred, tough as teak. Ludo writes unkindly of her that "she wore a pair of stout leather gauntlets, as if she had just returned from hawking," and Taylor tells us "She ate her ginger pudding casually, as if she were unconcerned with what it was." There is something heroic about her. Soldiering on is what she believes in. "Must keep going, she thought, as she so often thought." Back in Blighty, she doesn't stand a chance.

Mrs Palfrey at the Claremont is full of pairings. Begin anywhere, go anywhere, they are there. Burma and England. Past and present. London and the country. Ludo and Desmond, the pretend grandson and "*le vrai*," both, for their sins, as Ludo is once unable to stop saying, writers. Men and women—or, as it sometimes seems, especially to Osmond, the man concerned, man and women. (Even though at times the categories seem close to being reversed: "They lowered themselves into their chairs. As they aged, the women seemed to become more like old men, and Mr Osmond became more like an old woman.") Guests and staff. Summers and Mr. Wilkins. Paying commercial guests and long-stay residents. The Major and the Colonel. The sweet and tremulous Mrs. Post helping the birds build their nests with hair combings from her brush, and the actually rather redoubtable Mrs. Palfrey in her maroons (she *is* marooned) and her ends of fur (as a returnee from the tropics, no doubt she feels the cold). The one outing to see Mrs. de Salis and the other to a Masonic Ladies' Night. "The hallowed Launderama," also known as the Coin-Op Laundry; "the hallowed Chinese Lantern," and the "Ching-chong." The cheese counter at Harrods and Mr. Osmond's dream of settling down with Mrs. Palfrey in Suffolk somewhere and hosting, maybe, some "small dinner party, the odd cheese-and-wine set-to." Desmond's work in progress on Cycladic art and Ludo's stint waiting tables at the Plaka. The two "kept" women, rather ill-kept at that, Rosie and Ludo's mother. Find one of something, there'll be another. The taxis, the meals, the walks, the sparse, desperate things to look forward to. The books by Snow—the right Snow, or the wrong one. "Roast Surrey fowl or cold Norfolk turkey." This is what gives the book some of its playfulness, its depth, and its connection to fate. It means there is always the dream of being "set right" or "put to rights" or, best of all, "in the pink." Poor Mrs. Post, Emily or Last, "she got Elizabeth Bowen muddled with Marjorie Bowen, and could never remember that there were two Mannings and two Durrells and a couple of Flemings"— that would be double-o.... The wrong Elizabeth Taylor, and the right one. "'One can always read a good book twice,' Mrs Arbuthnot snapped. 'In fact one always *should* read a good book twice.'"

—MICHAEL HOFMANN

MRS PALFREY AT THE CLAREMONT

1

Mrs Palfrey first came to the Claremont Hotel on a Sunday afternoon in January. Rain had closed in over London, and her taxi sloshed along the almost deserted Cromwell Road, past one cavernous porch after another, the driver going slowly and poking his head out into the wet, for the hotel was not known to him. This discovery, that he did not know, had a little disconcerted Mrs Palfrey, for she did not know it either, and began to wonder what she was coming to. She tried to banish terror from her heart. She was alarmed at the threat of her own depression.

If it's not nice, I needn't stay, she promised herself, her lips slightly moving, as she leaned forward in the taxi, looking from side to side of the wide, frightening road, almost dreading to read the name Claremont over one of those porches. There were so many hotels, one after the other along this street, all looking much the same.

She had simply chanced on an advertisement in a Sunday newspaper while staying in Scotland with her daughter Elizabeth. Reduced winter rates. Excellent cuisine. We can take *that* with a pinch of salt, she had thought at the time.

At last the cab slowed down. 'Claremont Hotel' she read, as clear as could be, in large letters across what must be two – even, perhaps, three – large houses made into one. She felt relieved. The porch pillars had been recently painted; there were spotted laurels in the window-boxes; clean curtains – a front of emphatic respectability.

She hauled herself out of the taxi and, leaning on her rubber-tipped walking-stick, crossed the pavement and climbed a few steps. Her varicose veins pained her today.

She was a tall woman with big bones and a noble face, dark eyebrows and a neatly folded jowl. She would have made a distinguished-looking man and, sometimes, wearing evening dress, looked as Lord Louis Mountbatten might in drag.

Followed by the driver and her luggage (for the hotel gave no sign of life), she battled with revolving doors and almost lurched into the hushed vestibule. The receptionist was coldly kind, as if she were working in a nursing-home, and one for deranged patients at that. '*What* a day!' she said. The taxi-driver, lumbering in with the suitcases, seemed alien in this muffled place, and was at once taken over by the porter. Mrs Palfrey opened her handbag and carefully picked out coins. Everything she did was unhurried, almost authoritative. She had always known how to behave. Even as a bride, in strange, alarming conditions in Burma, she had been magnificent, calm – when (for instance) she was rowed across floods to her new home; unruffled, finding it more than damp, with a snake wound round the banisters to greet her. She had straightened her back and given herself a good talking-to, as she had this afternoon in the train.

In spite of long practice, she found that resolution was more difficult these days. When she was young, she had had an image of herself to present to her new husband, whom she admired; then to herself, thirdly to the natives (I am an Englishwoman). Now, no one reflected the image of herself, and it seemed diminished: it had lost two-thirds of its erstwhile value (no husband, no natives).

When the porter had put down her suitcases and gone, she thought that prisoners must feel as she did now, the first time they are left in their cell, first turning to the window, then facing about to stare at the closed door: after that, counting the paces from wall to wall. She envisaged this briskly.

From the window she could see – could see only – a white brick wall down which dirty rain slithered, and a cast-iron fire-escape, which was rather graceful. She tried to see that it was graceful. The outlook – especially on this darkening afternoon – was daunting; but the backs of hotels, which are kept for indigent ladies, can't be expected to provide a view, she knew. The best is kept for honeymooners, though God alone knew why they should require it.

The bed looked rather high, and the carpet was worn, but not threadbare. Roses could be made out. A corner fireplace was boarded up, but still had a hearth before it of peacock-blue tiles. The radiator gave off a dry, scorched smell and subdued noises. Heavy wooden knobs to the drawers of the chest, she noted. It was more like a maid's bedroom.

She took off her hat and pushed her hair about. It was short and grey and regularly waved, as if a hand had been spread over it and then squeezed.

The silence was strange – a Sunday-afternoon silence and strangeness; and for the moment her heart lurched, staggered in appalled despair, as it had done once before when she had suddenly realised, or suddenly could no longer *not* realise that her husband at death's door was surely going through it. Against all hope, in the face of all her prayers.

To steady herself now she sat down on the edge of the bed and breathed deeply, put up her chin as if she were setting a good example.

The lift, far off, whined. Soon, she heard its gate clashed to, and there was a scattering of sound, of footsteps, of conversation, people coming nearer, turning from one corridor into another. Two polite voices at last went by her door. She was grateful for them.

Her black mood had passed and she began to unpack. She hung up her clothes, and thought of erstwhile homes; but gratefully, not heart-brokenly any more. Everything she now touched was familiar – pills rattled familiarly in their bottles as she set them out on the bedside table. Her short fur cape she hung over a chair. It smelled of camphor and animal, as it always had. She decided to wear it down to dinner to create a decisive first impression. On whom, would be discovered, or not discovered. Beside her bed she put Palgrave's *Golden Treasury*, and her Bible, though she was not religious.

When she had unpacked – and she made it last as long as she could, so that later might seem sooner – she took her sponge-bag and went along the corridor to what was labelled on the door 'Ladies Bathroom'.

Her table was in a corner of the dining-room. It had a single white chrysanthemum and a sprig of greenery in a silvery vase. Soon it would have her own packet of crispbread and, at breakfast, her own Allbran and superior make of marmalade. She did not care for hotel marmalade.

At other tables sat a few other elderly ladies looking, to Mrs Palfrey, as if they had been sitting there for years. They were waiting patiently for the celery soup, hands folded in laps and eyes dreamy. There were one or two married couples who occasionally made observations across the table for appearance's sake, recalled to one another momentarily from a vague staring around or nibbling at bread. These seemed more in transit than the old ladies. The waitresses moved silently about on the thick carpet, as if assisting at a ritual. Many tables were empty.

After pasty celery soup, there was a choice of roast Surrey fowl or cold Norfolk turkey. Then the trolley was wheeled round with its load of wobbling red jellies, slopping fruit salad (mostly, Mrs Palfrey noted, sliced apples and bananas). Coffee was served in the lounge. It was all rather quickly over, with no conversation to eke out the time. Eight-fifteen.

In the lounge, knitting was brought out. There was even a little desultory conversation. Mrs Palfrey knew that in such hotels as this residents had special chairs and, in her usual way of being sure how to behave, on this first evening she sat down in a rather dark place by the door and in a draught, settled her cape about her shoulders and opened her Agatha Christie.

At nine o'clock, she noticed that people were on the move. Knitting-needles were jabbed into balls of wool (she would get some knitting for herself tomorrow, she decided), books were closed thankfully, as if they had been only intermission things, and stiff bodies got up with a fuss from easy chairs.

Mrs Palfrey alone read on, and was puzzled until an elderly woman, slower than the others, bent with arthritis and walking with two sticks, stopped her slow progress to the door by Mrs Palfrey's chair. 'Aren't you coming to watch the serial?' she asked, and she looked as if she might have smiled if she had not been in so much pain.

Mrs Palfrey got up quickly, and she blushed a little as if she were a new girl at school addressed for the first time by a prefect.

'My name is Elvira Arbuthnot,' the crippled woman said curtly, dragging herself away. 'We always like to look at the serial,' she said. 'It makes a break.'

Mrs Palfrey was satisfied with her first evening. Someone had spoken to her: she had a name to remember. Tomorrow, at breakfast, she could nod and say 'Good morning' to Mrs Arbuthnot. That would make a pleasant start to the day. And, afterwards, she would go out to buy her crispbread and pot of marmalade and some wool. (What on earth could she knit, she wondered, and for whom?) In this way, she would be busy all the morning.

She helped her new acquaintance to find a chair in the darkened room. She herself sat down on a hard seat behind a row of easy chairs. Heads with thinning hair rested on the antimacassars. Someone turned round stiffly and looked at her for a moment, as if warning her not to stir. She became very still. Of the serial she made very little, coming to it too late.

All night long the hotel was silent; even the London traffic seemed to be passing in another world, muffled and lulling. Mrs Palfrey slept badly and was glad when at last she heard someone going along the passage outside, and the sound of water being turned on with a rush. She got up and put on her dressing-gown and sat ready, sponge-bag hanging on wrist, waiting for the steps to come back. When they did, she was out of the door with discreet haste, and along the passage, and had her hand on the bathroom door before anyone else could even turn the corner.

The bathroom was warm and steamy, the floor mat was damp and in the wet bath was a coiled grey hair. She sluiced it out and tried not to think about it. She bathed quickly (out of consideration to others), her lemon-scented soap overcoming the earlier smell of carnations.

Later, dressed in her maroon woollies, her morning pearls and walking-shoes, she made her way to the dining-room and nodded just slightly to one or two people she passed on her way to her table in the corner. The elderly waitress stood glumly by while Mrs Palfrey hesitated between prunes and porridge, haddock and sausages.

As she waited for prunes, Mrs Palfrey considered the day ahead. The morning was to be filled in quite nicely; but the afternoon and evening made a long stretch. I must not wish my life away, she told herself; but she knew that, as she got older, she looked at her watch more often, and that it was always earlier than she had thought it would be. When she was young, it had always been later.

I could go to the Victoria and Albert Museum, she thought – yet had a feeling that this would somehow be deferred until another day. There was always so much going on in London, she had told her daughter, who had suggested Eastbourne as a more suitable place for her to live. In London, there were a great many free entertainments, and a great diversity of people.

Net curtains covered the windows of the dining-room, but she had a feeling that it had begun to rain again.

When she had finished breakfast, she went out into the vestibule and stood by the revolving doors, looking at the people scuttling by in the wet road, bowed under umbrellas, splashed by buses. Going to work. It was a proper Monday morning, Mrs Palfrey decided, and she went to the lounge, and began a cheerful letter to her daughter.

At eleven, she decided to brave it and set out to post her letter and do her shopping. This took up much less time than she had planned and, in spite of her varicose veins, she walked all round a neighbouring square. In the gardens in the centre were asphalt paths, a summer-house and dripping shrubs. The square was like a dogs' lavatory. All the pekes and poodles from the near-by blocks of flats had made their little messes by the railings. She had to keep an eye on the pavement.

I shall be able to watch the lilacs coming out, she thought. It will be just like the garden at Rottingdean. The setting could scarcely have been more different; but she felt a determination about the lilac trees. They were to be a part of her

8

rules, her code of behaviour. Be independent; never give way to melancholy; never touch capital. And she had abided by the rules.

At twelve o'clock she returned. She had been out an hour.

'England's manners!' cried Mrs Post, who came through the revolving doors after Mrs Palfrey. 'What has happened to them? They used to be so good.'

She dabbed at her gunmetal-coloured stockings, splashed by a passing car. 'No consideration.'

Mrs Palfrey clicked her tongue in sympathy.

'You arrived last night,' Mrs Post said – scarcely giving information. 'How long are you staying?'

Mrs Palfrey was purposely vague about this.

'I must hurry away and tidy my hair,' Mrs Post said, making for the lift. 'My cousin is coming for lunch. I have made this my home, you see; and all my entertaining has to be done here.'

As they went up together in the lift, a little constraint at first fell over them. They eyed each other's feet. At last, Mrs Post made an effort. 'Do you have any relations in London?' she asked.

'My grandson lives in Hampstead.'

'Oh, then, you will be seeing a great deal of *him*, I expect. It will make all the difference. Do you want this floor?'

They stepped out of the lift and walked along the passage together.

'Relations make all the difference,' Mrs Post said. 'Although one would never make a home with them.'

'Never,' said Mrs Palfrey.

'Hard as one's pressed. But I like to see them; I like them to come to see me. If it weren't for all my London relations, I do believe I should go to live in Bournemouth. The climate's milder, and there's always something going on.'

'I should have thought there was always something going on in London,' Mrs Palfrey said.

'It's true there is, but one just doesn't seem to *go* to it.'

2

As the days went by, went slowly by, Mrs Palfrey was able to sort out her fellow guests into long-term residents and birds of passage. The residents were three elderly widows and one old man, a Mr Osmond, who seemed to dislike female company and seldom got any other kind. He tried to detain in conversation the aged waiter in the dining-room, hung about chatting to the porter, waylaid the manager.

The bar was really only a part of the lounge where one pressed a bell and someone from the dining-room would come in time and unlock the cupboard where the bottles were kept. Here, at this end of the room, Mr Osmond sat in the early evenings. From the other end of the room came always the clicking of knitting-needles and the muffled hum of the Cromwell Road traffic beyond the heavy curtains.

Mr Osmond drank wine. He sat very still with the glass beside him as if it were keeping him company. He waited for the manager, who occasionally looked in. He could not hide his annoyance when Mrs Burton came down to his part of the lounge and kept pressing the bell for whiskies. She spent a great deal of money on whisky, which was a marvel to the other ladies – throwing money down her throat, Mrs Post said. She had other extravagances, such as mauve-rinsed hair, and what Mrs Arbuthnot always referred to as chain-smoking, although it was not. Mrs Arbuthnot, perhaps because of her arthritis, found it in her nature to be disparaging.

Mrs Palfrey, although deeply desiring to find her place and be accepted in it, had the strength of character to wish to make up her own mind about Mrs Burton. 'I speak as I find' might have been her motto, if she had not thought it servants' parlance.

The chief gathering-place for the residents was the vestibule where, about an hour before both luncheon and dinner, the menu was put up in a frame by the lift. People, at those times, seemed to be hovering – reading old church notices on the board, tapping the barometer, inquiring at the desk about letters, or looking out at the street. None wished to appear greedy, or obsessed by food: but food made the breaks in the day, and menus offered a little choosing, and satisfactions and disappointments, as once life had.

When the card was fixed into the frame, although awaited, it was for a time ignored. Then, perhaps Mrs Arbuthnot, on her slow progress to the lift, would pause nonchalantly, though scarcely staying a second. There was not much to memorize – the choice of two or three dishes, and the fact (which Mrs Arbuthnot knew, but Mrs Palfrey had not yet learned) that the menus came round fortnightly, or more often. There were permutations, but no innovations.

Mr Osmond would not condescend to join in the evasions

of the old ladies. He strode towards the menu when he thought he would, and stood manfully four-square to it and read aloud, and hummed and hah'd: would call across to the porter, 'Well I hope the bread-and-butter pud's better than last time. All watery. Bloody awful *that* was, take my word for it.' Man to man. It was rather strong language to Mrs Palfrey, and she frowned (before she, too, edged up). Her husband had never sworn before her, although she was sure he had often done so, at the right time, in the right place. She vaguely envisaged recalcitrant natives.

Mrs Burton hardly ever appeared for the menu-waiting. She had other things to do – such as pressing the bell. But on Mrs Palfrey's sixth evening, she happened to be passing through the entrance hall on her way back from the hairdresser's, and she and Mrs Palfrey, waiting for the lift together, took turns to read the menu. Mrs Burton sighed. 'Oh, the Friday fricassee,' she said. The lift came whining down, and they stepped into it. This was sometimes a means of making acquaintances, of striking up conversations, Mrs Palfrey had found. It was not good manners to remain glumly silent. 'Open to non-residents,' Mrs Burton quoted scornfully. 'That notice outside always amuses me. I doubt if anyone has ever been lured in by it.'

She had about her a strong smell of hair-spray and her lunch-time whisky. Her hair was mauver than ever, and she wore a net over it dotted with tiny velvet bows.

She had lived at the Claremont for five years, she explained, and very few non-residents had she seen stray into it. 'Nor have I seen a Friday without fricassee,' she added. 'The monotony! But they are all the same. Before this I was at the

Astor. Do you know the Astor? That's Bloomsbury. Ah, dear me, Bloomsbury! How very sad *that* can be on a winter's afternoon – especially Sunday. Now, why don't we have a little drink together before dinner?'

Mrs Palfrey, accepting the invitation, felt that the lift had really worked some magic, and she was quite excited at the thought of the stir she would cause – and not a stir of approval, she guessed – as she took her place in the bar with Mrs Burton.

Descending later, she tried to decide between a medium-dry sherry or Dubonnet. She felt both dashing and defiant. She wore one of her maroon dresses and it had a scattering of bead-embroidery across the chest. She had left her knitting-bag behind. With a slight flush, she walked to the far end of the lounge, and picked up an old, old copy of *The Field*. She turned the pages casually, keeping her head bent. Soon Mrs Burton came and pushed the bell with great authority. Staring at them across this part of the room was Mr Osmond. He had a glass of wine on the table beside him, but did not touch it. He sat patiently still, with his hands on his knees, as if waiting for the drink to drink itself.

Mrs Burton had removed her hair-net and filled the creases of her face with powder. Her face had really gone to pieces – with pouches and dewlaps and deep ravines, as if a landslide had happened.

'The drink has really taken its toll,' whispered Mrs Arbuthnot to Mrs Post at the other end of the room: but Mrs Post shook her head primly, although not in disagreement, counting stitches, her lips moving. When she had finished, she gave Mrs Burton a long, clear look, and shook her head again. 'It is very sad,' she said, as if out of her great compassion.

The waiter came at last, and Mrs Palfrey, having plumped for sherry, sank back to ride out the hostile interest from the other end of the room.

'My brother-in-law's coming to dinner,' Mrs Burton said. 'Hence the hair-do.' She gently touched it, but it did not yield. 'He keeps an eye on me, does Harry. Have you any relatives in London?'

She was not the sort of woman, Mrs Palfrey decided, with whom she would ordinarily have been in company ... not quite ... but life was changed, and to save her sanity she must change with it.

'I have a grandson who works at the British Museum. No one else. His mother lives in Scotland. No, I don't smoke, thank you.'

'Ah, you would have been nearer to him at the Astor. Will he be coming to see you?'

'Oh, yes. Desmond will be coming. He knows where to find me. We have always – had a link, d'you know. It is a relationship which sometimes skips a generation.'

'I like to see a young face.'

Mr Osmond had waylaid the waiter, who stopped – but impatiently – beside his chair.

'Something I thought would interest you ...' Mr Osmond mumbled. 'Suddenly occurred to me ... must tell Antonio ... on me travels ... Italy, it was ... your country ... frescoes ...'

The old pink face had a false, waylaying animation, for it was strenuous work holding his listener captive. Mrs Burton looked on dispassionately, pushing up her hair, for she could hear only snatches of his hurried, muffled talk: but suddenly Mr Osmond glanced across at her and said, 'Here must I lower my voice.' He half rose towards the waiter's sideways-bent head, and then shouted, as if the man were deaf '. . . the most enormous sex organ. Quite enormous.' Then he lowered his voice again, and said in a more intimate way, 'Frescoes. Italian frescoes. I gather you know what I mean.'

Mrs Burton had given a snort of laughter which she turned into a cough. Mrs Palfrey looked casually away and took a sip of sherry. So that's the poor old sort of man he is, she thought.

'Enormous!' Mr Osmond said again, and the waiter scuttled away. Alone, Mr Osmond sat very still in his chair and smiled. He had had his conversation.

'Dirty old fellow,' Mrs Burton whispered behind her hand-kerchief.

Silence from the other end of the room. Mrs Post was casting off stitches and Mrs Arbuthnot had retreated into her world of pain. Soon Mrs Burton got up and pressed the bell again.

At half-past seven, Mr Osmond was the first to stroll casually towards the dining-room, then came Mrs Arbuthnot moving slowly, looking spectral, step by painful step, with the two sticks inching along before her. She was like an injured insect. As she came to Mrs Palfrey – ignoring Mrs Burton – she paused. 'What have you done with that grandson of yours?' she asked. 'If we don't see him soon, we shall begin to think he doesn't exist.'

'Oh, he will come,' Mrs Palfrey said, and she smiled. She really believed that he soon would.

After dinner, she fetched her knitting and joined the others at the window end of the room, having made a stand to establish her personality. Mrs Burton returned to the bar with her brother-in-law, who was now the one to get up and press the bell and who looked as if he had done a great deal of it in his time.

3

Desmond did not come. The sweater Mrs Palfrey was knitting for him neared completion, and everyone knew that he had not come to claim it. Saving face had been an important part of life in the Far East, and Mrs Palfrey tried to save hers now. Trouble usually comes from doing so, and it came to her, for it involved her in telling lies, and in being obliged to remember the lies when she had told them. She had to invent illnesses for Desmond, and trips abroad connected with his work – which she knew quite well did not involve trips abroad. She found this a great strain, and along with it went her secret grief that she had no one of her own in London after all, and that the studious, rather prim young man she had always been proud of seemed utterly unconcerned about her. He had not even answered her letters, her invitations to dinner at the Claremont. Young men are always hungry, and very often hard-up, she had believed; but it was now clear that her grandson was neither so hungry nor so hard-up as to need any help along those lines from her.

She felt not only slighted, but indignant. A question of upbringing was involved. Letters should be answered. She could not help mentioning this lapse when writing to her daughter – 'just wondering', as only she was able. She often 'just wondered' or 'only mentioned' or 'merely suggested'. Her daughter made the lightest reference to this 'wondering', and in her usual bracing language, without apology or surprise. 'They're all the same. I've taken a scunner against the young.' She affected such Scottish words and they made her Scottish husband wince. He could not 'thole' them, as she would have put it.

Whether she reproved her son or not, Mrs Palfrey did not discover. He still neither came nor wrote, and she heartily wished that she had never mentioned him at the Claremont. She began to feel pitied. All the other residents had visitors – even quite distant relations did their duty occasionally; they came for a while, overpraised the comfort of the hotel, and went relievedly away. It was inconceivable to Mrs Palfrey that her only grandchild – her heir, for that matter – should be so negligent.

Mrs Arbuthnot, on one of her worst arthritis days, condoled with her spitefully, and that night Mrs Palfrey could not sleep. She fretted through the small hours, feeling panic at her loneliness.

I must *not* get fussed, she warned herself. Getting fussed was bad for her heart. She put on the light and took a pill, and wondered if the morning would never come. She tried to read, but her heart lurched so uncertainly that its throbbing rang in her head. At these times, she felt that anything would be better than being alone – a nursing-home, where someone else would be awake at night, even living with her daughter, supposing such had ever been suggested. In the morning – as she now promised herself – courage would return, the certainty that she would not give in. She would stay at the Claremont for as long as she could, and from there, at last, be taken to hospital and hope to die as soon as possible, with no trouble but to those who were paid to deal with her.

'The young are very heartless,' Mrs Arbuthnot had dared to say.

'He would come if he could,' Mrs Palfrey had replied, pressing her lips together, for they had trembled.

'We poor old women have lived too long,' Mrs Arbuthnot said with a smile.

Her very tone of voice when speaking of her husband, Mrs Palfrey had noticed, blamed him for dying, for leaving her in the lurch. He would have been so useful to her in the circumstances, have helped her to get about, fetched and carried: she might still have had a home of her own. But she was not alone like Mrs Palfrey. She had sisters who came and went, who sometimes called for her in cars and took her for drives, or to see her old friend Miss Benson in hospital. Miss Benson had lived at the Claremont before her illness.

'She had no one,' Mrs Arbuthnot said, meaning no one but Mrs Arbuthnot. 'Not a soul in the world. She was entirely alone.' Her eyes rested on Mrs Palfrey. 'No one ever came to see her. In all our years together here. Although she had been a well-known woman in her time.'

'I have been abroad a great deal,' Mrs Palfrey said. 'One gets out of touch.'

'One probably does. We need to keep our friendships in

repair. I think Doctor Johnson said that. But you, of course, you have your grandson.'

'Yes, I have Desmond.' I am not really like that poor Miss Benson, she assured herself. To Mrs Arbuthnot she explained, 'My daughter is so far off, in Scotland.'

'And you wouldn't care to live in the North?' Mrs Arbuthnot asked, probing.

Mrs Palfrey had not been invited to, and she did not get on well with her daughter, who was noisy and boisterous and spent most of her time either playing golf or talking about it. 'I doubt if I could stand that climate,' she replied. In London, the rain was pouring down: in Scotland, it was coming down more steadily, as snow. They had watched it on the television that evening.

'No, of course not,' Mrs Arbuthnot said quietly, with her eyes on Mrs Palfrey once more. They were such very pale blue eyes as to make Mrs Palfrey uneasy. She thought that blue eyes get paler and madder as the years go by. But brown eyes remain steady, she decided, with a little pride.

In some desperation (for she had not yet discovered that her fellow guests talked a great deal more about visitors than was warranted) Mrs Palfrey wrote to one of her old school-friends, who lived in Hampstead. She knew her address, as they had exchanged Christmas cards for sixty years, although that was perhaps hardly what either Mrs Arbuthnot or Doctor Johnson would have called keeping their friendship in repair.

Mrs Palfrey invited Lilian Kibble to luncheon at the Claremont and Lilian Kibble, thinking that Hampstead to the Cromwell Road was too expensive a taxi-ride, replied that she would love to and very soon would drop Mrs Palfrey a line, suggesting a date – which Mrs Palfrey thought she might have done equally well at the time of writing. Of course, she heard no more from Mrs Kibble, but for a week or two she allowed herself to hope for a letter. It had always been an uneven friendship. Mrs Palfrey had been the staunch, good, unexciting school-friend to whom Lilian had returned again and again after her skirmishes – those raids upon others' 'best friends', quarrels which followed, passions for mistresses, jealousies and betrayals. She had gone out of Mrs Palfrey's life after school, apart from the Christmas cards; but had had three husbands, Mrs Palfrey knew, and still had one of them.

Another old acquaintance from Foreign Service days lived in Richmond. It was rather a long way from the Cromwell Road; but all the same Mrs Palfrey decided to try to rustle her up. She wrote to her, too, and invited her to lunch – but the poor creature was in even worse case than Mrs Palfrey, was lying immobile of a broken hip. She did not, however, suggest that Mrs Palfrey should go out to Richmond to see her. Mrs Palfrey thought she should have done, and would have gone.

After that, she could think of no one else to invite. She had learned a little at the Claremont and she did not make the mistake of telling Mrs Arbuthnot that her friend Lilian might be coming to lunch one day. She began to feel more and more like poor Miss Benson.

Time went by. It could be proved that it did, although so little happened.

At the Claremont, days were lived separately. One sat at separate tables and went on separate walks. The afternoon outing to change library books was always taken alone. Mrs

Arbuthnot could not venture so far, and Mrs Post went for her, and nearly always brought back the wrong book: she got Elizabeth Bowen muddled with Marjorie Bowen, and could never remember that there were two Mannings and two Durrells and a couple of Flemings. 'So kind of you to take the trouble,' Mrs Arbuthnot would thank her, laying the book aside.

Mrs Palfrey felt quite elated when Mrs Arbuthnot – her usual slave having a cold – one afternoon asked her to change her book at the library. It was like being back at school again and asked to run an errand for the head girl. She was just going out for one of her aimless walks, to break up the after-noon, and was delighted to be given an object for it.

'Something by Lord Snow, perhaps,' Mrs Arbuthnot said. 'I cannot stand trash.'

'But if you've already read it . . .' Mrs Palfrey began ner-vously.

'One can always read a good book twice,' Mrs Arbuthnot snapped. 'In fact one always *should* read a good book twice.'

Mrs Palfrey took the rebuke quite steadily. After all, Mrs Arbuthnot was the one who was doing the favour. She set off, resolved to bring back such a treasure – the very latest Snow, perhaps, – that Mrs Post would have lost the job for ever. She knew that in thinking this she was behaving like her erst-while friend Lilian, but was dogged about it. (Lilian would have been defiant.) The Claremont was rather like a reduced and desiccated world of school. Of course, the food was better; but, for grown-ups, would have been uneatable if it had not been.

*

It was beginning to grow dusk as Mrs Palfrey, triumphantly clasping the latest Snow, returned from the library, from one quiet and now familiar street to another. A drizzle blurred lights and slimed pavements. She walked slowly, feeling tired, keeping close to the railings of areas. Basement windows in those streets were lit up and some had curtains still undrawn, so that she could see – though a little ashamed of looking – the interiors of rooms, sometimes bleak kitchens, sometimes cosy sitting-rooms with a tablecloth laid and a bird in a cage.

How dreadfully the veins in her leg ached, so that putting one foot in front of the other was pain each time; but she had passed the afternoon well, and there was only sitting down ahead of her, a long evening of just sitting and resting. She could not have spent the whole day doing that. The walk had taken her out of herself, as well as out.

Suddenly – she could not afterwards remember how, her ankle turned, or she skidded perhaps on the greasy pavement – she stumbled, tried to save herself and fell with the sickening crash of a heavy, elderly person.

At first, she felt only shame. She struggled to recover herself, her dignity, although the street was at that time empty; there were no passers-by to see her sprawled there. She felt shaken – the breath shaken from her – and afraid. Every heartbeat threatened to be her last. She dragged herself up by the railings and leaned there, trying to quieten herself. I shall never get home, she thought, and tears, from her shocked dismay, threatened.

She was scarcely aware of a door opening in the area below the railing. Light streamed out across wet stones and ferns and a dustbin, and up the steps a young man came, hurrying. He took her in his arms and held her to him, like a lover and without a word, and a wonderful acceptance began to spread across her pain, and she put herself in his hands with ungrudging gratitude.

She felt blood making its way slowly down her leg, but dared not look.

After a time, the young man propped her against the railings while he picked up her handbag, the library book, her walking-stick; then he put his arm round her shoulders – she was taller than he – and helped her slowly down the steps. She went without protest, because there was nothing else to do, and she was glad to be got out of sight, and the possibility of being looked at lumped against the railings, disorganised, disorderly. If he would give her a glass of water, she could take one of her pills from her handbag, collect herself and make a plan.

'I'm sorry!' she gasped, sitting down in the room. Her lips, all her face felt numbed and drained of blood.

'I shouldn't talk yet,' he said. He went away and came back with a cup of water and it was as if she had no need of words. She pointed to her handbag and he brought it, unclasped it for her and held it open, kneeling before her. Then, seeing her torn stocking and bleeding leg, he went away again and came back with a bowl of warm water and a dirty towel. She was rather shocked by the sight of the towel, but this shock came too soon after a greater one to make much difference, and she submitted. She was completely in his hands and glad to give herself up. She felt no sense of outrage when he lifted her knicker elastic over her suspenders and unfastened her stocking. Most tenderly he swabbed her knee and dabbed it with the dirty towel. She felt no pain. Her leg seemed not to belong to her. He fetched a handkerchief from a drawer and tied it round her knee, drew up her torn stocking again and then sat back on his heels and looked up at her and smiled.

'I could make you a cup of tea,' he said.

'I couldn't give you so much trouble.'

He seemed to consider this, then said, 'It wouldn't be *much* trouble.'

'You have been so kind.'

'Yes, I'll make some tea,' he said, having decided. 'My name, by the way, is Ludo. Ludovic Myers. Rather something, don't you think?'

'And mine is Palfrey – Laura Palfrey,' she replied, feeling so much better.

'Then we both have ridiculous names,' he said, getting up and going to fill a kettle.

Never in her life had she thought Laura Palfrey a ridiculous name, but she was not at all cross. She even smiled.

'How far do you have to go?' he asked.

'To the Cromwell Road, the Claremont Hotel. Do you know it?'

'No.' He looked amused at the idea of knowing the Claremont Hotel. 'I can get you a taxi, if you like,' he said. 'It shouldn't cost too much from here.'

'I should be so grateful,' she said, feeling exhausted.

At last she was able to take in her surroundings – a bare deal table with books, a gas-fire turned low, a dark suit hanging on the back of the door. The curtains did not meet properly across the window and were pinned together with two large safety-pins.

'It was lucky I was here,' the young man – Ludo – said. 'I had only just got back from work. Was just pulling the curtains together.'

'Where *do* you work?' she asked, making an effort at conversation.

'In Harrods.'

The kettle began to sing on the gas-ring, and he brought out a tin mug for himself. The mug had a Union Jack printed on it. The young, Mrs Palfrey had noted often with surprise, had a passion for the Union Jack. All those long-haired, long-skirted girls seemed to carry Union Jack carrier-bags. She had wondered if they were sincere – and if it was quite suitable even so.

'Which department of Harrods?' she asked.

'Oh, no, I don't work *for* Harrods. I work *at* Harrods. In the Banking Hall. I take my writing and a few sandwiches there. It's nice and warm and they're such comfortable chairs. And I save lighting this gas-fire, which eats up money. Milk?' He held up a bottle, and she bowed in acceptance. The bottle was half-full and had a curdy deposit up its neck.

'You are a writer?' she asked.

'Well, at present that's what I'm trying to be, although I *have* had other jobs.' Gallantly, but reluctantly she felt, he turned up the gas-fire, stood staring down at it, his hands round his mug of tea. Such eyelashes! Mrs Palfrey thought – they threw a long shadow down his cheek-bones, and when he turned to smile at her, she thought his face mischievous, crinkled by a slight smile; his eyes narrowed considering her, almost as if he had hit on a joke to play on her. The word 'glee' came to her mind. There was glee in him, and she was both fascinated and uneasy.

'I am keeping you from your writing,' she said, putting down her cup. Her knee was beginning to hurt, and she was worried now about that dirty towel.

'I've been working all day. I told you that, Mrs Palfrey ma'am,' he said. 'Now I'm going to have a little read and open a tin of something.'

He was obviously hard-up and hungry, as she had wistfully thought her grandson might have been.

'You have been so kind,' she said. 'But now I feel that I could make a move.' She shifted her leg stiffly.

'Then I'll pop round the corner and whistle up a cab.'

He drained his mug and made off. She heard him tearing up the area steps and along the pavement. Listening to his footsteps dying away, she sat back and thought of her adventure, and she went on to imagine him after she had left here, turning down the gas-fire and opening a tin of something.

Presently she heard the taxi draw up and Ludo running down the steps. She had her speech all ready. 'I should be delighted if you would have dinner with me at the Claremont one evening. I should like to repay your kindness in some way.'

He looked quite astounded at the idea – really appalled; and then the look of glee came back into his eyes.

'Well, that would be very grand,' he said.

'Would Saturday suit you? On Saturday, there is usually a rather better menu.'

'Saturday would be lovely.'

He helped her up the steps and into the taxi and when it had driven off, he returned to his room and, leaning over the table, wrote in a notebook 'fluffy grey knickers ... elastic ...

veins on leg colour of grapes ... smell of lavender water (ugh!) ... big spots on back of shiny hands and more veins – horizontal wrinkles across hands.'

Then he turned down the gas-fire and began to open a tin of spaghetti.

Mrs Palfrey managed to get to the lift without meeting anyone. She went to her room and felt sick and shaky, unsticking the handkerchief from her knee and seeing the damage for the first time. She was a long while putting herself to rights. Her leg throbbed, and stiffness was setting in.

When at last she came down to the lounge, Mrs Burton had already rung the bell and Mrs Arbuthnot was waiting impatiently for her library book.

'I had begun to think you were lost,' she said.

'I'm afraid I had a fall on my way back and had to bathe my leg.'

'It looks as if my library-book has had a fall, too.'

'I'm sorry. I dropped it. But I have tried to sponge it.'

'Well, it was none the less very kind of you. Are you all right now?' Mrs Arbuthnot asked the question lightly, as she began to turn the leaves of the book.

'Only a little stiff. All the same, I think I shall have a glass of sherry before dinner.'

She limped towards the bar, and Mrs Arbuthnot watched her go, as if to a damnation of her own choosing.

When he had finished the spaghetti, Ludo took his suit from the back of the door and went round to the launderette. Under the harsh light, he sat and wrote up some notes, describing a young man sitting alone in a launderette at night. Sometimes, he stared gloomily across at his suit turning slowly over and over in the dry-cleaning machine, which looked as if it were trying to digest it, and would have disgorged it if it could.

4

On Saturday evening, Mrs Palfrey put on her best beaded dress and sprinkled lavender-water on her handkerchief. Before going downstairs, she took a sealed envelope from a drawer and slipped it into her handbag. Although her movements were slow and deliberate, she felt flurried and anxious.

It was on Thursday evening that she had told the waiter – well within Mrs Arbuthnot's hearing – that she expected a guest to dinner on Saturday.

'So your grandson is coming to see you at last,' Mrs Arbuthnot had said on her slow way past Mrs Palfrey's table and, for some reason she searched for later, Mrs Palfrey let her go without a word.

It was the first time since she had become a widow that she had been involved in an untruth. In fact, since early childhood, she had not lied at all except on her husband's behalf – to get Arthur out of cocktail parties which he abhorred, or to stave off importunate natives when he was tired. Now – by omission – she was trying to get away with what she thought of as a whopper, and she wondered if either she or Ludo would be equal to it.

He had seemed ready enough to fall in with her; had had no scruples as she herself had; had thought it all rather a lark.

She had tracked him down in Harrods Banking Hall. He was reclining in his comfortable chair, beautifully warm – and it was a bitter, gusty afternoon – scribbling away, oblivious to the slack or tense resting bodies about him. Nervously, Mrs Palfrey approached him, stood before him and coughed. His eyes, when he raised his head, seemed still to be viewing another world, an inner world in which he had been alone.

'I am sorry to interrupt you,' Mrs Palfrey said, more put out than ever by his dazed look.

He stood up then, with a fan of papers in his hand. He smiled.

There was a vacant chair next to him and she sat down and began to speak of her plan in a low and hesitant voice. He soon grasped what she was suggesting and took her side at once against Mrs Arbuthnot and her dreaded condescensions. 'I let her go without a word,' Mrs Palfrey said. 'And now it is too late.' She looked about her at the resting shoppers, and felt a deep embarrassment at what she had had to say; but it was nothing to the humiliation Mrs Arbuthnot would have had her suffer. In just being with Ludo, she felt a certain ease.

He had listened to her with a curious expression on his face, as if he could not believe his ears: his eyebrows had shot up and stayed there. He was almost beautiful, she thought, and the idea so alarmed her that her glance flew away from his face and fastened on one of his shoes, as it swung back and forth, the thin sole flapping.

'We will keep ourselves to ourselves,' she promised. 'It is just in case I am obliged to introduce you – in passing, you know. They are rather an inquisitive little set. Is it too much to ask? Or must I go back and make some explanation to Mrs Arbuthnot?'

'Goodness, no! I shall enjoy myself no end.'

'At seven-fifteen, then. I shall be sitting in the lounge. We will have a glass of sherry before dinner.' She flushed a little at her sophistication, at the idea of entertaining this young man, and of their shared guilt. She stood up and held out her hand. Once more, he bunched up his papers and got to his feet. 'I shall call you Desmond,' she said.

'Christ!' was all he had replied.

Mrs Palfrey, crossing the lounge towards the bar, felt herself watched. But not by Mrs Burton, who was with her brother-in-law again, laughing and drinking and heedless of anyone else.

It was the shoes Mrs Palfrey was now worried about. She had seen the dark, respectable suit hanging on the door in Ludo's basement room, and was easy in her mind about that. But those old shoes he had worn in Harrods, with the sole hanging loose from one of them ... suppose he had no others.

Her fears were realised. He had no others. He came into the lounge and almost fell headlong – that flapping sole curling back as it met the thick carpet.

His composure was amazing. He led everyone's eyes away from his feet, by his gesture of outstretched arms towards Mrs Palfrey. She panicked, fearing lest he might overact his grand-filial role; but, with just the right touch of fond familiarity and respect, he came forward and kissed her lightly on her cheek. At the same time, he registered the strange, tired petal-softness of her skin, stored *that* away for future usefulness. And the old smell, which was too complex to describe yet.

Mrs Palfrey, unwilling for him to wander about on this hazardous carpet, got up herself and pressed the bell. Returning to her chair, she bade him sit down.

'What would you like to drink, Desmond?'

'Whatever is suitable under the circumstances,' he said in a low voice; then, bending nearer to her, asked, 'Who is that old codger over there, staring at me like crazy?'

'I will tell you later,' Mrs Palfrey said, avoiding Mr Osmond's eye.

It was all going with a swing. There would be so much to discuss at dinner. She had had qualms about it; that he would be glum and young and regretful; but now she was under the influence of charm – a new ingredient in her life. The unmended shoes were an eccentricity. She glowed.

'Will you bring two glasses of sherry, Antonio,' she said to the waiter. 'I think medium-dry. Is that all right for you, Desmond?'

Ludo bowed his head.

Mrs Palfrey had murmured those words to herself, going about her bedroom earlier, getting ready: 'medium-dry' she had said with an air of sophistication, staring at herself in the glass and bringing the biggest pearl exactly centre-bottom of the necklace.

'And may I have the menu and wine-list?' she added, having also rehearsed that.

The waiter, in the way of looking surprised, put his thin

mouth sideways. In this hotel, guests looked at the menu by the lift, or in the restaurant quietly awaited what they expected. À la carte was a farce.

Ludo leaned back easily, but his eyes were darting to and fro, noting everything, noting Mrs Arbuthnot noting him, and Mrs Post, in her sad pot-pourri colours, fussing over her knitting.

'Over there is Mrs Arbuthnot,' Mrs Palfrey said, in a low voice to Ludo. 'With the sticks.'

'I thought so. I shouldn't be afraid of her, you know. Although you seem very much the new girl round here.'

'Of course. Mrs Arbuthnot has been at the Claremont for years.'

'It has entered her soul.'

'But we aren't allowed to die here.'

He threw back his head and laughed.

'But isn't that sad?' she asked doubtfully.

'I don't see anything sad about you,' he said. He thought, I mayn't write it down; but please God may I remember it. We Aren't Allowed to Die Here. By Ludovic Myers.

Mrs Post hurried by, slightly ducking her head by way of greeting. Sherry was brought, and Mrs Palfrey handed the menu to Ludo. 'We can go à la carte, if you like,' she said recklessly.

While he sipped his drink and studied the menu in silence, she began to urge smoked salmon upon him. She was nervously aware that Mrs Arbuthnot was slowly approaching on her way to the dining-room. When she reached them, she paused. 'So you have your grandson at last,' she said to Mrs Palfrey, but looking at Ludo, who stood up quickly, pressing down the sole of his shoes.

Although not even glancing at Mrs Palfrey, Mrs Arbuthnot sensed nervousness in her when she introduced her grandson. She wondered about it, while making a remark or two to Ludo. He seemed to her a quite presentable young man, in spite of the state of his footwear. Educated they all knew he was.

'Is the British Museum open on Sundays?' she asked him.

'Oh, yes, it is one of our busiest days,' Ludo said smoothly, and Mrs Palfrey felt a surge of admiration and relief.

'I should like to hear more about it,' Mrs Arbuthnot said, and again she felt Mrs Palfrey's tension – a sudden alteration in breathing and a quick ducking of her head. 'But now,' she said, 'I must go in to dinner.'

She inched her way towards the door.

'Jesus!' said Ludo. 'I rather see what you mean. Those wicked old eyes.'

'She is often in great pain,' said Mrs Palfrey.

'We shall have to have our wits about us,' Ludo said. 'As a matter of fact, I think I'll have soup and then the veal,' he said, kindly choosing from the *table d'hôte*.

'Well, it might be quicker,' Mrs Palfrey said.

Going in to dinner, she took his arm; but this was so that she might steady him if he tripped again, not to lean on.

'Well, Grandmamma,' he said, looking about him and smiling as he unfolded his napkin, 'I really am awfully hungry.'

Desmond had always called her 'Grannie', and she had never liked it, for it seemed a name for some mumbling, toothless crone. 'Grandmamma' made her sit up straighter.

She smiled back at him and said in a low voice, leaning forward, 'So far, so good.'

They were drawn together by their complicity. She had known, after the first hesitant moments of her embarrassment in Harrods, that her deception – their deception – must be treated lightly – as rather a lark. So Ludo had described it.

Mrs Burton's laugh burst out heedlessly at intervals. Her brother-in-law sat back, smiling at the power he had to amuse her.

'She's having a high old time,' said Ludo.

'Yes. Mrs Burton is rather sophisticated. She drinks a great deal, and goes out a lot and spends goodness knows how much at the hairdresser's. She practically *lives* there.'

'It must cost quite a lot to stay here,' said Ludo in a careless tone.

'Yes, it does. Quite an amount.' She looked across the table at him, and he knew that the conversation was closed. All these rich old ladies, he thought.

He drank his soup, ate his veal with a kind of hungry concentration, which was a great pleasure to Mrs Palfrey. She was doing something for him, as he was doing something for her, and when he lifted his glass to her, she felt – for the first time since she came to the Claremont – that she was envied and respected, knowing herself watched from other tables. The waitresses moved about the room like sleep-walkers.

'The portions are not large, I'm afraid,' she said, when he had put his knife and fork together on his empty plate. 'I suppose they are meant for frail old stomachs.'

'Marvellous food,' he said happily. 'I've never enjoyed myself more, with my clothes on.'

He said it automatically as he continued to butter and ravenously eat bits of bread.

She flushed, unnoticed by him, and signalled to the waiter to refill his glass. She felt up and down about Ludo – uncertain, then sure – as she had felt when, so long ago, she had fallen in love with Arthur: in those earlier days before she had become quite sure.

The waiter brought some dull-looking pieces of cheese and Ludo cut off hunks from them while Mrs Palfrey sat back; unable to eat any more, but vicariously enjoying his great appetite.

'The Camembert is wonderful,' he said. It was really, as she knew, a remaining chalky inch or two, off the rim of some Brie. She smiled and nodded.

With great care, he buttered a little biscuit, balanced a piece of cheese on it and held it up to her. He dodged it about before her laughing mouth, her protesting fluttering hands and then deftly popped it between her teeth.

'You will have your grandmother awake with indigestion all night,' Mrs Arbuthnot said from grimacing lips as she passed their table on her way out of the room. Mrs Palfrey, swallowing the biscuit, felt that she had made an exhibition of herself, or had been made an exhibition of.

Ludo pulled a face at Mrs Arbuthnot's back as she limped away, and again Mrs Palfrey was not sure – not at all sure.

'She was quite kind to me on my first night here,' she said. 'When I was feeling rather low. She asked me to go down to the television room. One doesn't forget those things.'

She suffered a little flurry of unpopularity when she asked for their coffee to be served at the table, and by the time it was brought the dining-room was empty save for a couple of glum strangers, and Mrs Burton and her brother-in-law laughing their heads off and drinking brandy. So Ludo and Mrs Palfrey could talk more easily, no longer fearful of being overheard. Once or twice, earlier, they had made mistakes – Mrs Palfrey telling him things which, as her grandson, he must have known already, and he, speaking disrespectfully of his mother, forgetting that she was supposed to be Mrs Palfrey's own daughter. She had hushed him; but for the sake of seemliness, not expediency. In their different ways, both were too candid for the game.

'I don't take sugar,' she said. He stirred several spoonfuls of it into his coffee. 'But I used to like it,' she said as if she were excusing herself.

'Good for you.' He went on stirring his coffee, and then suddenly looked up and smiled.

She had a feeling that they were talking in different languages – each only half-learned by the other. She had never felt this with Desmond; and knew no more young people.

'I think that when we have finished our coffee, I will see you off, if you don't mind,' she said. 'There is not much point in going back into the lounge to run the risk of being asked a lot of questions.'

'No, I suppose we shouldn't push our luck.'

'And you have your writing to get on with. I mustn't take up too much of your time.'

She suddenly felt tired: exultant, but tired. She longed now to be alone, to be pottering about her bedroom, getting ready for bed, and going over the evening in her mind.

'Here is your handkerchief,' she said, taking the envelope from her bag. He looked puzzled. 'When I cut my knee,' she added.

'Is it all right? Your knee, I mean.' He put the envelope in his pocket and cast a glance over the table. Nothing left on it to eat. 'Well, this has set me up for the next week. It was terrific.'

'I hope you will come again one day,' she said anxiously.

She saw a look of uncertainty on his face, and glanced quickly aside.

When she had seen him off, she went to the lounge and sat down for a while, waiting for the effects of coffee to wear off before she went to bed. Mrs Burton and her brother-in-law had returned to the bar. Sometimes when he had made her laugh, she gave him a little push with her elbow. Mr Osmond sat staring in front of him, his hand rising and falling on the arm of his chair as if to some music only he could hear. Mrs Arbuthnot pettishly turned the last pages of the latest Snow; then snapped the book shut. 'Whether it's me or not, I don't know; but it seems to me he's going off,' she said, and then, more directly, to Mrs Palfrey, 'Your grandson seemed to enjoy his dinner.'

'He seems to enjoy everything,' Mrs Palfrey said happily.

'And makes such a fuss of you,' Mrs Post said in a wistful voice.

'He has always been very affectionate.'

'A good-looking young man.'

'Oh, he reminds me so much of my husband. When we first met.' Mrs Palfrey was shocked at herself for saying this.

'Really?'

'Yes, it is almost uncanny.'

'Stuffing you with biscuits,' Mrs Arbuthnot said, suddenly, angrily, unable to bear any more of Mrs Palfrey's complacency. She leaned forward and slowly massaged her swollen knee.

'Yes, he's such a tease,' said Mrs Palfrey.

'I suppose now he's at last turned up we shall be seeing a lot of him.'

'I expect so,' Mrs Palfrey said with a perceptible (to Mrs Arbuthnot) air of unease.

Mrs Post knitted away; her lips moving. For some reason, one of her ears was stuffed with cotton wool. She finished a row, looked up with a glazed expression, said, 'Yes, a nice-looking lad', and returned to her pattern.

That night, Mrs Palfrey was the first to go to bed.

When Ludo reached home, he was cold; for he had no overcoat. He decided to allow himself the luxury of half an hour's gas-fire before going to bed, and he knelt before it rubbing his hands. When he was warm, he fetched a notebook and opened it and began to write. It was headed 'Exploration of Mrs Palfrey'. He wrote steadily for a while: racked his brains, frowning, then suddenly jotted down, 'We aren't allowed to die here'. Then he put away the book and began to undress. He found the envelope in his pocket and opened it. Inside the laundered handkerchief was a folded five-pound note and a little card on which was written in a large, surprisingly actressy scrawl, 'Thank you for your kindness.'

Mrs Palfrey slept well, and all night, and her lips were level, as if she were about to smile.

Half-way through the night, Mrs Arbuthnot gave up hope of sleeping. Her rigid limbs were torture to her, and every attempt at finding a more comfortable way of lying hurt. She switched on the light and decided to make another onslaught on C. P. Snow. But she had lost the thread and could not be bothered to try to pick it up again. She blamed Mrs Palfrey for bringing the book, and the author for writing it.

She sat staring about the room. It was the same shape – small shape – as Mrs Palfrey's. Her husband would have complained to the management, and with effect. In those days, she had been apprehensive when he did, being a most uncomplaining person herself. Now she had come to complain all the time: and with no effect at all. She saw, with a three-o'clock-in-the-night flash of ghastly clarity, that she complained about things only to underlings like herself, who could do nothing. Her husband went, as he had liked to say, straight to the fountain-head. She was afraid of the fountain-heads. Her husband – so busy being bossy – had left her comparatively badly off; and the fountain-head was concerned only with making the hotel pay. He – they – stuffed elderly women into the worst bedrooms at a price they could just afford; because one-night guests (extra laundry bill) would have made a fuss.

Mrs Arbuthnot was humble to the fountain-head for another reason. The time was coming, she knew, when she would no longer be able to manage for herself, with her locked and swollen joints, and so much pain. The Claremont was the last freedom she had left, and she wanted it for as long as she could have it. She knew the sequence, had foreseen it. Her total incapacity: a nursing-home then, at more expense than the Claremont, and being kept in bed all the time for the convenience of the nursing staff. Or going to stay with one of her sisters, who did not want her. Or – in the end – the geriatric ward of some hospital.

Can't die here, she thought, in the middle of this night. And there might be years and years until *that*. Arthritis did not kill. One might go on and on, hopelessly being a nuisance to other people; in the end, lowering standards because of rising prices. For her, the Claremont was only *just* achieved. Down the ladder she obviously would have to go.

And now she began to think most bitterly of Mrs Palfrey – with all that wine-drinking, and her flushed cheeks, and the young man to whom she had offered smoked salmon at five-and-sixpence a portion. They had leaned towards one another over the table, their eyes on one another's faces, like lovers. Later, buttering a piece of bread – he had eaten so much butter that the waiter had grown sullen – he had said (Mrs Arbuthnot straining her ears): 'Mummy's a bit of a slattern; that's putting it mildly.' 'I can't let you speak of your Mamma like that,' Mrs Palfrey had replied – and had immediately laughed, as if it were not her own daughter she should be defending. Mrs Arbuthnot had ears sharpened by malice, and she sat at a near-by table; but this was almost all that she had heard, although her head had ached with listening.

Mrs Palfrey is a dark horse, she thought. At this unintended little pun in her mind, she tipped her head back against the pillow and grimaced, by way of smiling. 'You're a dark horse, Mrs Palfrey', I shall say. She turned her head to look at the clock, and there was a sound like the crushing of granulated sugar at the back of her neck as she moved it. Now she needed to make a journey to the lavatory down the corridor. So many times a night she must grasp her strength for this ordeal. She deferred, and drowsed and slept.

5

On Sundays – especially p.m. – Ludo was always depressed. Something lowering was in the air: at least three times during the day, for instance, the dreadful clanging doom of neighbourhood bells, the sauntering, church-people's legs beyond the area railings. He squatted and squinted up at them, at the boring hats of the women going by – they were mostly women – and he was enraged with them for so lowering his spirits. They did so to the extent that he could not work: and he could not *go* to work.

From somewhere – most certainly not from his mother – he had inherited a feeling that Sunday was a day of rest, and so he fretted through it, and always came to the end of it with a sense of wide ennui and wasted time.

Sometimes, during this particular Sunday, he thought of his five-pound note, and was tempted to go out to spend it; but he did no more than walk to a pub at midday, where he knew no one, met no one. To be lonely in South Kensington on a Sunday was the utmost loneliness, he decided.

In the afternoon, from duty, he wrote to his mother. 'Dearest Mimsie' – grimacing as he wrote the word. This was to him simply a Sunday-afternoon task, going back so long – to pre-prep. school, he supposed. He could remember himself as a little boy in that bleak, battered playroom, drawing the letters laboriously on the page. 'Dear Mimsie.' Sometimes a tear had fallen. So, from the beginning, he had hated Sundays. And those early ones had probably been the worst ones of his life.

'Dearest Mimsie,' he wrote now. 'Thank you for the postal-order.' (For it was still like school.) 'I really live sparsely now, and it made – the postal-order, I mean – briefly, the difference between starvation and survival. I am working hard at my novel, and, to reward me, I suppose, fortune cast an old lady down my area, just when I needed her, for it took my fancy to write about elderly women. I used to watch them in the boarding-house when I was in Rep in Woodbury, sitting like toads in dark corners, dropping off or dozing, or burrowing down the sides of armchairs for knitting-needles. It is an exercise of the imagination for me, but, all the same, I was glad enough to be able to examine a real old lady once more at close quarters – a rather fine example of the species. It is lonely here. In your love-nest, you never could imagine the Sou-Ken loneliness of Sunday afternoon. I imagine you and the Major flirting over the crumpets, having a delicious time, licking your fingers of the butter, making one another laugh. Whereas, my treat, is to go out soon to the launderette, and then wait impatiently for Monday.' (He was really writing to himself.)

'I have never been able to manage a Sunday. Even when I

was in Rep, and busy. There is really no escaping it. One has, at some time, to go out into the streets, and there are all the West Indians going to chapel in hideous hats and spectacles – even the tiny girls have felt basins on their heads, and gloves. I never saw *you* wear a hat or gloves in all my life. I'll say that for you. My Mrs Palfrey I was telling you about was bare-headed; but she wore a pair of stout leather gauntlets, as if she had just returned from hawking.

'I did, more or less save her life, and she gave me £5.' (He scratched out '£5', and wrote above it instead 'dinner at her hotel'.) 'Not your sort of scene; but I was so bloody hungry, having spent your nice postal-order on baked beans and getting my suit cleaned. (Perhaps your Major has some old suits. I should not be at all offended to receive one; for I have to trim mine with nail scissors before I go to work.)

'She has bad legs, Mrs Palfrey.' Then he thought that he was going on too much about Mrs Palfrey, and he was bored with it, and had been trained since early days not to bore his Mimsie. He tapped his forehead with his pen, half closed his eyes, went into a yawning daze, and suddenly wrote, 'with love from Ludo', and was done with it.

Something now to do. He could go out and post his letter. He crammed into a polythene bag one sheet, two shirts, two pairs of pants and some towels, and then, for a reason he did not know, suddenly decided to unpin the curtains and take them down. They had a strange, musty smell. He pushed them into the bag and set out.

The streets were as dull as ditch-water. He decided that, when he had finished his novel about how dull they were, he would go to live abroad, where even (for he had been to Spain

46

with Mimsie) the Sunday bells sounded better, and the cold was drier.

The launderette (coin-operated) had overhead fluorescent lighting, which enabled him to read easily his George Gissing.

Next to him, in the before quite empty launderette, came and sat down a young girl. The little patent leather shoes with straps, he first noticed, peering over, down, from his book like an old man. One of the tiny shoes went to and fro impatiently. The tights were white. Still from under his lids, his eyes travelled slowly up, over the slim white knees, to a hem of dusty black velvet. Ludo hoisted himself up in his chair, read another paragraph, and then glanced more frankly across at the top of her head, making a show of bored yawning, wristwatch winding. Her long hair was straight, and dyed an old woman's grey. Her pale face was touching in its unhealthiness, the mournful eyes, the colourless lips. She was staring ahead of her.

'Quiet tonight,' he said.

'Don't bother to chat me up,' she replied.

At the Claremont, the Sunday passed. It could be said to have passed, decided Mrs Arbuthnot. It was another Sunday wrested from the geriatric ward, she told herself. And why? what for? she wondered. What has it *been* for?

Mrs Burton, in a new fur hat, went to church. Mr Osmond, after a word from the hall porter, retired to do up his fly-buttons and also went to church. Roast beef and Yorkshire, and snoozing over the colour supplements. A dread lethargy. Soon, tea. Tiny cucumber sandwiches which repeated, as Mrs Post kept saying, tapping her bird-cage chest.

Mrs Arbuthnot had been taken for a little drive, and now, in the evening, sat pale and anguished. Her sisters had, with difficulty, shifted her about a little, so something had been achieved. She had had a breath of fresh air, a change of scene, and was supposed to be better for them both. Her sisters were certainly better. They were, at the moment, having a nice drink, flushed with relief, and the knowledge of duty done.

Mr Osmond listened to the weather forecast, with a transparent hand, like a shell, curved behind his ear. He was disgusted – not so much by the future weather as by the accent it was read in. He kept snorting and turning his head in annoyance. 'I don't want a damned Aussie telling me about my English weather,' he complained. '"Minely derigh!" I should have thought there were plenty of wholesome English girls who could have done a simple job like this. Minely derigh!'

'Well, it will be a nice change from the rain,' said Mrs Post.

'They never speak the truth,' Mr Osmond replied.

Later, they made a move to the television room and, after the serial, stayed on for the news and the demonstration. There was usually a demonstration on Sundays, with milling crowds in Trafalgar Square and forays into Downing Street. The policemen and the horses were always sympathised with. They had the Claremont solidly behind them. 'Oh, those poor horses!' Mrs Post kept exclaiming. 'What have they ever done to deserve this?'

'Long-haired louts,' Mr Osmond said from time to time.

Mrs Palfrey, with her new stake in youth, said nothing. She was confident that Ludo would never shame her by carrying a banner, or throwing a paving-stone. He seemed to believe in nothing, and she was glad of this.

After the demonstration, united in their disgust of it, they returned to the lounge, and peace. There were strangers, booked in for one night only, on their way somewhere, properly whispering, sitting in a corner, drinking coffee.

Soon, there was the soft, slapping sound as Mr Osmond shuffled a pack of cards for a game of patience: against this, the knitting sounds, and sighs, and stomach gurglings (quickly coughed over).

'Well, another Sunday nearly gone,' Mrs Post said quickly, to cover a little fart. She had presence of mind.

'Now don't you wish your life away,' warned Mrs Burton; but she tapped her bright finger-nails against her teeth, from boredom; and she yawned and yawned until she thought her poor jaw would give way,

Mr Osmond laid out the cards slowly. He had bony, shiny hands, with whorled wrinkles above each joint.

'Ho, ho, ho!' yawned Mrs Burton, holding nose and chin together for safety – might dislocate her jaw. Then she wiped her eyes, suddenly burdened with, defeated by drink. 'I'm for beddy-byes,' she said at last, struggling to gather herself together.

'It is three thousand days ago today that my wife died,' Mr Osmond said, to no one in particular.

'Birmingham,' said Ludo.

'Birmingham what?' asked the girl in the white tights.

She turned her head a little – bored concession.

'That's where you come from. I've just been trying to place the accent.'

'I happen to come from Pinner.'

'I adore the way you say "Pinnah".'

'I didn't say "Pinnah".'.

At least they were having a conversation, he thought.

'Is that in the Harrods' delivery area?'

'I simply don't know *what* you're talking about.'

She said 'what' with a great whirring sound, as if to emphasise Pinner.

'It *is* rather important,' he said.

'Important? I suppose you're a director of it,' she said, looking down languidly, chin on hand, at his broken shoe.

'No. In all fairness, I am *not* a director,' he said. 'But it is my place of work.'

'Oh, Christ, you bore me,' she said. 'I told you not to chat me up. How many more times?'

'Doris,' he said presently, as if talking to himself. 'Mabel. No, Edith.'

She could not help saying, 'Mabel, Edith what? Or are you mad? Talking to yourself.'

'Trying to guess your name. You look quite like a Mabel to me. I settle for Mabel.'

'Do you *know* what someone called Mabel looks like?' she asked in a dangerous tone.

'I told you, I am only trying to guess.'

'If you *must* know, my name's Rosie.'

'Well, Rosie, from Pinner, where are we going for a drink?'

'You rile me,' she said, turning one shoulder. 'And what's more you get on my nerves.'

'My name's Ludovic. Ludo.'

'You have to be joking,' she said automatically.

Presently, in the silence in which they were sitting, he had an idea. He took from a pocket Mrs Palfrey's five-pound note.

He smoothed it carefully and, holding it by one corner, dangled it in front of Rosie. 'Do you know this trick?' he asked. As she did not answer, he went on quickly, 'You'd think it quite simple. You'll probably think *me* simple for suggesting it. But you'd be surprised. All you have to do is to catch it when I let go, and if you can, you keep it.'

She looked at him with astonishment – her first change of expression from disdain.

'Come on!' he said coaxingly, as if to a child. 'Just snatch at it with your little paw.'

He let go of the note and she caught it between thumb and finger and stared at him uncomprehendingly. Then she resumed her disdain and he in his turn looked astonished.

'I've never seen that happen before,' he said.

She held out the note to him, waving it impatiently, to be rid of it.

'No, no, it's yours,' he said. 'That was the bargain. All the same, I couldn't be more amazed. Perhaps it was because you were sitting down. Not to make any difference to its being yours, but to satisfy my curiosity, see if you can do it again.'

'Oh, belt up,' she said. She flicked the note in his direction and went over to the spin-dryer with her polythene bag.

He was about to lose her.

'Let's go to the Chinese,' he said desperately, when she turned towards the street door. 'Rosie,' he added pleadingly.

From habit she assumed a look of heavy boredom, of protective scorn; and then – 'Rosie!' he said again, softly – something in her face faltered, the drooping lines of it wavered, as if against her will. There had not, so far, been much variety in her expression, but here at last was something new. It was hunger, he thought.

A rather noisy little band of commercial travellers had invaded, quite late, the lounge of the Claremont. They were gathering overnight for a conference in the morning, and some uneasiness and false *bonhomie* hung over them as one after another (and there was sometimes a good-humoured scramble), they got up to ring the bell for the waiter. Antonio came grudgingly, and in the end stood about, holding a tray, waiting to serve the next round.

The little band of regulars had gone to bed, which was as well; for of them only Mrs Burton could have borne the noise. She had been in one of her deep sleeps for an hour; only a parched mouth would awaken her.

Mrs Palfrey lay and listened to the murmur of a married couple in the next room. It was unrhythmical and intermittent, an exchange grown casual and homely over the years. She knew – looking back – how precious it could be, though not valued at the time. *His* low voice sometimes ran along with *her* lighter more floating one, speaking at the same time, and then for minutes they fell silent, moved about the room, opened and shut drawers: things were put down, dropped; furniture pushed about. The two were settling in for the night, peaceably, and at their accustomed pace; and Mrs Palfrey, hearing them, felt lulled and comforted.

'It was really my week-end for going home,' Rosie explained, stripping a spare-rib neatly with her sharp little teeth. 'But my parents have gone winter-sporting.'

She had become less laconic in the darkness of the restaurant, with its stretches of shadow and painted dragons and tasselled lampshades. So different was it from the glare of the Coin-Op Laundry.

'Every *other* week-end,' she went on, screwing her greasy fingers into her paper napkin, 'I go down there to stoke up for the next week. It's worth the fare, because I eat like crazy. Roast beef and Yorkshire. All those things I loathed when I lived there. And I pinch great slabs of fruit cake out of the larder.'

She now dabbed at her glistening chin with the shredded napkin. 'They live in another world,' she said: and Ludo realised that this covered everything – all the differences in age and outlook. Her parents would not have understood that, for the girl flat-dwellers, clothes came before food; fun before comfort; privacy nowhere. To him, the priorities were reversed, with privacy first, the assuagement of hunger next (which was different from having a meal), and clothes last. The Chinese supper was instead of buying a new pair of shoes, as he had intended, and guessed that Mrs Palfrey hoped.

'Yes, they live in another world,' he agreed, keeping things going, while Rosie ate the last spare-rib. 'My mother has a love-nest in Putney. She is a sort of kept woman.'

'So?' was all she said, beginning at one end of the bone and going fast up to the other, as if playing a mouth-organ. 'Only sort of?' she asked, when she had finished. She leaned back and sighed. 'Kept woman, I mean?'

'She does a part-time job as a receptionist; but I think the Major pays the rent.'

'Another world,' sighed Rosie, looking round and putting a

finger-nail between two teeth, grimacing, then sliding her tongue about her mouth. 'They never had any fresh ideas, did they? Oh, sweet and sour pork, how super!' Her eyes flew fast from dish to dish, as the waiter arranged the table. 'I'm sorry I was rather shirty in the coin-op,' she went on, 'but truly I thought you were a bit etcentric'

'Try again,' he urged her. 'I just can't understand it.' He took the five-pound note from his pocket and held it once more in front of her.

She put thumb and finger nearly together, leaned forward ready, and he saw the note flutter down to the carpet.

'That's how it's meant to work,' Ludo said, satisfied at last, bending to pick up the note.

'Crispy noodles I dote on,' she said, with a rapt and solemn look as if she were in church.

'Well, I'm glad of that, about your not catching it, I mean. Now you won't think me quite so "etcentric", perhaps.'

'Maybe not,' said Rosie, and she looked up at the Chinese waiter and her smile, rising from the corners of her lips, spread all over her face, seemed to lift her into the air. 'Oh, water-chestnuts!' she said softly, looking up into his pouchy eyes.

But water-chestnuts are expensive. They were sliced thinly and scattered only sparsely over the chicken. Rosie sorted them out with her chopsticks, savoured them. 'They're so inscrutable,' she complained. 'They never say anything or listen.'

'It's a texture quite on its own,' Ludo said, and he picked out all of his water-chestnuts and spooned them into her bowl. 'Nothing else quite like them.'

'Absolutely nothing,' she agreed, accepting his share, looking thoughtfully into her bowl. 'But what about you?'

'As a matter of fact, my need isn't as great as yours. I had a very good dinner last night.'

'Where?'

'At the Claremont.'

'I never ever heard of it.'

'No, I don't suppose you did. I was invited there by an old lady I picked up.'

'You're a great one for that.'

'Literally picked up, I mean. Off the pavement. She'd had a fall.'

Rosie wasn't interested in old ladies falling about, or in Ludo's chivalry. 'What does your mother look like?' she asked, finding the subject more to her liking.

'She has bags under her eyes. Auburn hair, dark at the roots most of the time. Nice figure.'

'Well, that's something.'

'Those sort of smart clothes you get from Jewish Madam shops; but somehow there's the impression that all is not well beneath – you know, one imagines grubby shoulder-straps, sordid old roll-ons. Can't think why it is. But one does.'

'Jewish Madam shops? Sordid roll-ons! I *must* say. Where d'you get all that from?'

'I'm a writer,' he said, leaning forward. 'Or . . . I am about to be a writer. I mean, I am *already* a writer, but . . .'

'I thought we were talking about your mother,' she said, in a voice from which patience was ebbing fast. 'You know, and her sordid roll-ons. I didn't know such things existed still. But I'd have thought this Major wouldn't have cared much for all that. Where does he get his money from, anyway? My uncle was a Colonel, and he never had a halfpenny.'

'No, this one of my mother's is only one of those wartime Majors, but I think he rather fancies being called it, so he kept it on. He's really in steel. Something in steel.'

'He must be old.'

'Why?'

'From that war.'

'I suppose he's sixty-odd.'

'Don't! It makes me squirm.' She squirmed.

'You don't like old people?'

'I don't choose to think about them.'

'You'll be old yourself one day.'

'Why order all this food and then put me off it?'

'What about your parents?' Ludo asked.

'Oh, they lark about in their way,' she said. 'They give awful drinks parties, with about a hundred people standing jam-packed, shouting at one another. Sometimes on a Sunday morning when I'm there I go round with a tray of stuff – pretend caviare on toast and all – and some of the men are quite *awful*, and the women say, "Oh, how *pretty*", meaning the caviare and the bits of lemon, and the American ones say, "My, and *some* one's been busy around here". They're so bright and shouty, and hateful to me, really; because they know their old men are squinting down my dress at my bosom.'

'But you haven't got a bosom.'

'And shall keep it that way, thank you. I suppose your mother has one of those enormous ones sticking out of her Jewish Madam clothes.'

'You seem strangely fascinated by my mother. I told you she had a good figure.'

'By whose standards? The Major's, I suppose. But what

about your father?' she asked, and she helped herself to more fried rice.

'He got very tired, and died,' Ludo said.

'Oh, sorry!' Rosie said vaguely – even rather crossly, as if she wished she had not asked. 'This rice soon got cold, I must say.'

'I did my best. With my father. Tried to buck him up a bit. If you don't praise people just sometimes a little early on they die of despair, or turn into Hitlers, you know.'

'Do they?' Rosie asked.

6

Even for some time after her fall, Mrs Palfrey was too stiff to walk far, so that she found the days passing slowly. She often thought of Ludo and her pleasant evening with him, and wondered if he would ever come again, and felt that he would not. For he had been vague, had not left open the way to her renewing of the invitation. He had had a look of uncertainty – or reluctance – when she suggested it. The machinery for carrying on their acquaintance did not exist, though constant reference to him by Mrs Arbuthnot and Mrs Post unfortunately did.

'If we went to the British Museum should we see him?' Mrs Post asked, dangerously, had she but known it. The last thing she had ever imagined herself doing was endangering somebody, in which she was quite unlike Mrs Arbuthnot.

'Oh, no,' Mrs Palfrey said quickly, 'he is tucked away in the archives.'

'Fascinating,' said Mrs Post.

Mrs Palfrey, feeling flustered, took herself off on one of her brief outings – just as far as the Square, where there were little hard buds on the lilac trees – she guessed they would be that boring pale mauve when they blossomed – and there was an unfolded crocus or two coming up from the black earth. There was also a bitter wind, which tired her and seemed to set rigid all the down-going folds of her face.

It was late afternoon, a time of day which depressed her. There were now, there were beginning to be, little glimpses of domesticity through lit but not curtained windows. She could glimpse bed-sitting rooms – like Ludo's, some of them – where once cooks had attended ranges, rattling dampers, hooking off hot-plates, skimming stock-pots, while listening to housemaids' gossip brought from above stairs. Mrs Palfrey went slowly by, imagining those days, which were almost clearer to her than this present structure of honeycomb housing and the isolation of each cell, because they were the days that belonged to her being young, and so were the clearest of all to her.

Some of the basement windows were covered by vertical iron bars, so that it must be like being in prison to live behind them, she thought. One could peer up at feet going by, and the wheels of cars; but no sky, only the stuccoed wall of the area, the dead leaves blown there, a fern growing out of a crack in the plaster, or moss covering bricks; dustbins; or a row of flower pots containing old earth, but no longer anything growing.

But there was life stirring below stairs and, occasionally, a hint of cosiness. Smells of cooking came up: a man rose from a sagging wicker chair and yawned, stretched: blue-white television sets flickered in otherwise darkness: plates were being dealt out on a cloth-covered table.

Mrs Palfrey gave herself a little rest, re-settling her old furs on her shoulders. She glanced down sideways at a lit-up aquarium in a room below her, at the black and golden fish weaving back and forth. Rude old woman, I am, she thought, smiling.

But the grit swirled about the pavement in this unkind wind, a piece of newspaper wrapped itself round her ankle, and she poked it away with her stick and went on.

In the back basement of a small hotel, she saw a boy cutting the rinds off rashers.

Arthur and I, she suddenly thought, would come back from our walk as it was getting dark, and he would carefully put little pieces of coal on the fire, building what he called 'a good toast fire'. She could picture his hands with the tongs – a strong, authoritative hand, with hair growing on it. If I had known at the time how happy I was, she decided now, it would only have spoiled it. I took it for granted. That was much better. I don't regret that.

After their hard, often uncomfortable, sometimes dangerous married life, that retirement – the furnished house in Rottingdean, had, simply, been bliss. They became more and more to one another and, in the end, the perfect marriage they had created was like a work of art. People are sorry for brides who lose their husbands early, from some accident, or war. And they should be sorry, Mrs Palfrey thought. But the other thing is worse.

She walked towards the Cromwell Road, and it was quite dark now with the stillness of fog settling down. Back at home . . ., she began to think, and then checked herself. She stumped on grimly. It had come to her naturally – that the Claremont was home.

*

Ludo sped along the Brompton Road, going home from work. All about him the lights were blurred and shaggy, hanging in the mist. The rush hour. And it was the stale time of the year, between Christmas and spring, and nothing new about it that he could ever find: it was an end, not a beginning.

Everytime he saw a pair of white boots flashing towards him, or standing in a bus queue, he thought of Rosie. In the middle of the day, he had gone for a walk, shrugging off stiffness. He passed and repassed the boutique where Rosie worked, he peered through the windows. It was teeming with the Sou-Ken flat girls, trying things on in their lunch-hour. Beatles beat forth. 'Wednesday morning at five o'clock when day begins . . .' Plaintive, beautiful. Shifting, coloured lights rayed the ceiling. He had entered, and hidden behind a rail of P.V.C. coats, his eyes on Rosie.

A middle-aged woman, who seemed to have strayed here by mistake, emerged from a dressing-room, looking battered, frantic, at the end of her tether. She unloaded on to Rosie an armful of garments. 'The jackets are too big and the skirts too tight,' Ludo heard her say. 'Well, I don't suppose you expected just to walk into something, did you?' Rosie said coolly. When the woman had gone, slinking out into the street, Rosie said, but without much rancour, 'Silly bitch', and began to hang up the clothes.

'Bo!' said Ludo, coming from behind the coats.

'Oh, *you!*' she had said, with an air of great weariness.

Indescribably delicate was her aloofness, her way, Ludo remembered – going along past the darker space of Brompton Square – her way of saying 'You must be *joking*', or '*Do* you *mind*' – so faintly, hardly said at all. Her beauty, and that untroubled air she had, made all the pert and worn-out phrases seem newly minted on her lips.

Going westwards was going away from the bright shop-lights. In the Cromwell Road there were shadowy patches of pavement, and darkness high up in the buildings against which the sky was a lighter, bruised colour. He passed the Claremont quickly, almost guiltily, as if his grandmother really *were* in there, waiting forlornly for a visit from him.

He turned off into a dimmer, quieter street, then into another, passed the hallowed Launderama and the hallowed Chinese Lantern, dived into a corner pub and bought two bottles of light ale, then hastened on to open and warm some spaghetti hoops. Rosie was coming to supper.

He thought – had begun to think in Harrods when his mind should have been on other things – that, after the first baiting splurge at the Chinese, they would have to begin again as he meant to go on – as he needs *must* go on; although he was far from sure that Rosie had the slightest intention of going anywhere, with him.

He thought – pinning the curtains together – that the evening would prove something.

At the last moment, hearing her footsteps, he lit the fire.

Mr Osmond was writing to the *Daily Telegraph*, as usual. 'We are lucky to have such a fine body', he wrote, 'of men', he added, after taking a sip of wine.

Mrs Palfrey, depressed, watched him. Action, she thought. He is taking action, he is expressing himself, keeping himself going. Some indignant thought made him give a little snort. She, for her part, did nothing, but sat with her hands in her lap. Her walk had left her tired, but in a fidgety and not a lulled way. She wished that she could look forward to bedtime with a hope of real rest then, as once she had. She wrenched her mind away from thoughts of other days, and turned her head sharply.

'Well!' said Mrs Post, coming with her workbag to sit near by. 'You really *do* look a little fagged. It's this cold wind, perhaps.'

She was too vague, too bird-brained to achieve real kindness. She had always meant well – and it was the thing people most often said about her – but had managed very seldom to help anyone. Yet this evening, unintentionally, she was to help Mrs Palfrey, who was sitting there idly playing with her heavy rings, looking up at her dully.

'You finished your knitting,' Mrs Post said. 'I hope your grandson was pleased with it.'

'I quite forgot to give it to him. It's still in the drawer upstairs,' Mrs Palfrey said. Then, lowering her gaze to stare at the carpet as if at a thought slowly taking place, 'I quite forgot,' she said again.

'Oh, well,' Mrs Post said easily. 'He'll be back again soon, I'm sure.' She withdrew into her own world, arranging her hands about her knitting, settled, began to click the needles together. Mr Osmond ostentatiously closed his eyes, then covered them with his left hand, obviously trying to concentrate.

As they rose, one by one, to go in to dinner, a party of middle-aged people there for a mild celebration, all instinctively sat up and straightened their backs. They tried to look more alert, and to forget their future.

Mr Osmond closed the door and followed Mrs Palfrey at a

distance; remembering an old, old risqué anecdote, he told it to the manager, *en passant*.

Silence, almost, in the dining-room. They lowered themselves into their chairs. As they aged, the women seemed to become more like old men, and Mr Osmond became more like an old woman.

7

On a Saturday afternoon, knowing that the Major would be at Twickenham ('Twickers' he called it, 'Rugger at Twickers'), Ludo went to Putney to see his mother.

Perhaps from his father he had his sense of duty, and from his mother its sporadic quality. She still – even now – seemed to feel a little of it towards him, occasionally sent him a birthday-card of sick humour, or a funny anecdote to write into his novel: once, had pressed on him a pair of the Major's socks she could not be bothered to mend. They were a mustard yellow. 'Perhaps really fit only for Oxfam,' she suggested doubtfully. 'Oh, they'll come in,' he had said cheerfully, unable to hurt anyone. Even in disposing of them, he had hoped they would come in. Some tramp or drop-out might peel them off the gilded railing-points outside the Garibaldi Hotel, and be glad of them.

'Just dropped in as I was passing,' he said, when his mother opened the door of the house in Putney. (And he thought, I rather doubt if we've ever said anything true to one another since I was about six, and learned better.)

He followed her up the stairs to her flat on the first floor: her rump slid from side to side as she went, but under control, not floppy. As he must not cram his mind with useless details, he tried to ignore her appearance. He was paying a call, merely.

The sitting-room was beautifully warm to him – warmer than Harrods, even – with focal points of heat from two electric fires, and no damp coming out from anywhere, as it always did at home, after ten minutes of the gas-fire. Used as he was to basement darkness or artificial light, he was charmed by windows filled with white sky and branches.

'How's himself?' he asked.

'He's gone to a football match. I expect they're all boozed by now. They stand about in the car-park, drinking out of boots.'

'You can't be serious.'

'I mean, they keep their bottles in the boots of their cars. And seem to go from one to the other – like a pub-crawl.'

'Ah, yes.'

'It sounds rather like a point-to-point meeting.'

'You talk a very strange language, Mimsie.'

'Do I, darling? Then let's talk about you instead. How is your novel coming along?'

'They don't do that. They have to be pushed a bit.'

'I'm sure.' She sat down in a sagging chair, and from it leaned forwards and began to pick things off the floor – bits of newspapers, and chocolate papers and some sewing things. A frowsty little love-nest, Ludo thought.

'I really,' she began ... 'No, I shouldn't say it. I should've said it right at the start, and I'm sure I did. But, not that I'm interfering . . . I only wonder – I did just wonder – if switching boats midstream is sensible. Oh, I really loved you being an actor. "My son's on the stage", I used to say, and everyone was thrilled and dying to hear more.'

He wondered to whom she had said it: for she seemed to have no friends.

'I was hardly ever on the stage once the curtain had gone up.'

'But every great actor started that way. I'm sure Sir Laurence did his stint. You lack his patience and his perseverance.' She smiled, as if to make this seem a bit of a joke.

Ludo believed that patience and perseverance were his two strong points.

'Besides,' she added, more to the point, 'it's so lonely, just sitting there scribbling away, day after day. And it lacks glamour.'

One of her favourite words. No one else he knew ever used it. Kept woman though she was, she had none of it herself.

'What does the Major think about it all?' he asked. He shuffled his fingers about in a near-by box of chocolates, but came on nothing but empty paper cups.

'I wish you wouldn't call him that.'

'Everyone else does. In the pub, they shout out "Hows' tricks, Major? What's the Major having?"'

'I think he would like it if you called him Dickie.'

'Then I *will* try to remember. After all, it makes no odds to me.'

'Well, what Dickie thinks is that it's up to you, of course.'

To keep out of the way, Ludo thought. Which I do.

*

The porter saw Mrs Palfrey across the Cromwell Road. She was always nervous of the fast traffic, especially with a bulky parcel under one arm. It was this speed and noise which put Bournemouth in her mind from time to time, where there could be quiet roads, and seasonal terms, too, which at the Claremont, though advertised, meant very little. 'And during the Motor Show, when there's not a bed to be found in London, they positively hate us,' Mrs Arbuthnot had said.

'That's good of you, Summers,' Mrs Palfrey said, when they reached the other pavement.

It had been good of him; for, at the top of the steps, backed by the manager, some new arrivals waited for a taxi. In such cases, the manager thought that the residents must look after themselves. Summers dashed back, and then kept making dangerous little forays into the road, waving his arm; but it was always difficult for cabs along this stretch.

Saturday afternoon seemed a heartless time of the week to Mrs Palfrey, and made no better by the approaching gloom of Sunday. The callous traffic swept down the Cromwell Road and crowds poured into and out of Gloucester Road station, like bees about a hive. The young sped by – sometimes shying from her slow progress only just in time, carrying their Union Jack bags full of groceries, or their arms full of French bread for the Saturday-night parties.

She was glad to turn off the busy road. In these side streets no one was about. It was a strange, dead world. No sound came from the houses: nothing was happening.

Mrs Palfrey was trying to walk off a stiffness in her hip, but it would not be walked off. It seemed, instead, to be settling in, locking her joint, so that every step was consciously achieved. She realised that she never walked now without knowing what she was doing and concentrating upon it; once, walking had been like breathing, something unheeded. The disaster of being old was in not feeling safe to venture anywhere, of seeing freedom put out of reach.

Her fall had deepened her uncertainty. And there was no husband to take her arm across a road, or protect her from indignity when she failed. I can have a little rest when I get there, she promised herself. And perhaps he will offer me a cup of tea.

But when she did get there, Ludo was out. It was Saturday afternoon, and Harrods – in those days – was shut. She had felt certain of his being at home.

It was bitterly cold – 'raw', as Summers had put it – and when she had knocked on the door a second time, she stood in the area for a minute or two, sheltering against a damp wall. She dreaded her homeward journey and the recrossing of the Cromwell Road.

She set down her parcel by the door, wrote a note for Ludo, and pushed it under the door, as there was no letter-box. In the dingy, late afternoon light, she could see how neglected the house was, with flaking paint and peeling plaster. It was probably years since anyone had cleaned the basement window.

There's nothing for it, she thought grimly. She had to get back, and there was only one way of doing it. The afternoon had turned out differently from how she had imagined it, and what had seemed at one time a good idea, seemed now to have been a foolish escapade. But if I can't take half an hour's walk, she thought fretfully, and set her lips together and shook her head a little.

Up the steps she plodded. At least now she was free of her parcel. I might see an empty cab, she thought; but this was really only an encouraging talking to herself, for one never did see an empty cab when it was desperately needed.

In Hereford Square, some of the trees bore tiny buds. She realised that she had never desired the spring as she desired the one ahead. It would bring, she believed the end of her aches and pains, renew her freedom, lift her spirits. She was talking to herself again. She kept these thoughts going, and her feet moving, and the young hastened past her with Saturday night ahead of them, and all that that entailed. It was in their eyes, their walk, the swing of their hair.

I feel like an orphan, Ludo thought, going home. I'm quite alone, and might as well face it.

His mother had continued gently to deplore his having left the repertory company; but she had done it in a vague way as if simply trying to show interest in and give advice to a stranger. At four o'clock she had toasted him an early crumpet, leaving, he noticed – having followed her to the little kitchen – seven others for her to share with the Major when he returned from Twickers. When she had done that, she had begun to get restless. She went off and changed her dress, came back and plumped up cushions which badly needed it; she blew some dust off the top of the clock and checked its time with her wrist-watch; she carried away the empty chocolate-box.

'I hope they won,' she said.

'Who was playing?' Ludo asked.

'I'm afraid I've forgotten.'

In her impatience, she had not toasted the crumpet enough, and Ludo thought that eating cold tripe might be rather similar, though possibly less harmful.

'You don't drink tea, do you?' she had said, as if she knew something about him.

He walked round the room while he chewed, went and looked out of the long window at a little paved garden below.

Why do I bother? he had wondered, wishing that he had not wasted the fare just to be made so unwelcome and probably get indigestion. At that point, as if guessing his thoughts or, more likely, trying to urge him on his way, she had rummaged in her handbag and fished out a crumpled note. Eyeing it hopefully, he had none the less thought, Even her pound notes look scruffy.

'You can buy something for your supper,' she said. 'For I can't imagine what you're living on, not having a job.'

Before she could begin again, he said, 'What with Grannie's money, I think I'll be able to manage for another month or two. I don't spend much, but every little helps.' He put the note in his pocket and moved to the door. He had been paid off, and it was only fair to go. He thought of a nice parcel of fish and chips, and then a long stint at his novel.

He was still thinking of work when he came out of the Gloucester Road station and saw all the young people milling about, beginning to get busy about their Saturday-evening pleasures, gathering noisily like the starlings in Trafalgar Square at dusk: all the air was full of their jostling excitement. He thought wistfully of Rosie, and imagined her coolly preparing herself for the fray.

Feeling – and it was unlike him – a little sorry for himself, and the loneliness he had himself imposed, he tucked his warm parcel of fish and chips inside his jacket and hurried down the road, keeping his hands in his pockets.

And someone had called on him, although no one ever did. For a wild moment, when he picked up the lumpy parcel, he thought of Rosie, and knew at once there could be no reason for doing so. Inside, on the doormat, was Mrs Palfrey's note.

It was a very nice sweater, he decided. Because he was cold, he put it on at once. The sleeves were a little too long, but no matter. Really, he was quite touched, and pleased and grateful, too. I must do something about her, he thought vaguely. Go to see her. Or perhaps write. Yes, write. Writing's best. He began to lift things, looking for a stamp.

8

At the beginning of March, there were a few still, sunny days; for the month, as usual, came in like a lamb and would, no doubt, go out like a lion.

There were other signs of Spring – mauve crocuses out in the gardens (the starlings had shredded the yellow ones to pieces) and a faint haze of buds on some of the trees.

Mrs Post put her small hair combings out of the window – London birds, she had read, were short of nest-building materials.

Summers set out two folding chairs at the top of the flight of steps, and on one of these Mr Osmond would sit, looking down at the traffic, and with a word for everyone who came and went. He was crowned with glory in these days, for the tail-end of one of his letters to the *Evening News* had been printed. It was about foreigners receiving free medical treatment in England, which he personally was not prepared to subsidise. He carried the clipping about in his note-case. 'What about this, eh?' he had asked the manager, had pointed with a shaking finger at his name – R. Osmond, Claremont Hotel, London, S.W. 'Not a bad little advertisement for you.' Mr Wilkins's smile had been inadequate, Mr Osmond thought. It had not shown gratitude. 'Of course, they left out the best part,' he said, 'about the doctor I was forced to have attend me in Paris. But I believe that is their wont. I have a copy of the original letter if you would care to read it.'

'Some time, some time,' Mr Wilkins said, and he clicked his fingers at the hall porter whose attentions he required more than Mr Osmond's.

There were other signs of winter's being over than crocuses and garden chairs. Mrs Palfrey felt better in herself, as she put it when writing to her daughter, and twice a day she was able to take a little walk in the hinterland of the Cromwell Road, or she sat for a little while on one of the seats in the gardens of the Natural History Museum, watching the pigeons.

And Lady Swayne arrived from the Cotswolds on her annual visit. Mrs Palfrey had not met her before, but she was well known to the other residents. About this time every year she came to London for various affairs of business and pleasure, to have the dentist go over her old grey teeth, to see Parson & Gunnell, her solicitors, to get her corns pared, be measured for shoes, and to buy elastic stockings in Wigmore Street. She inflicted herself on old friends, and went to the theatre. About the Claremont she condescended dreadfully, and talked of staying at Brown's Hotel in erstwhile days.

'Not to worry though,' she said robustly. 'It's cheap and cheerful here.'

After all, thought Mrs Arbuthnot resentfully, 'it's our *home*,' and title or not, she considered Lady Swayne had bad manners.

Mrs Palfrey, the others noticed, was rather gathered in by Lady Swayne, who was pleased to find someone new to admire the photographs of her elegant grandchildren, and of her garden in Burford with its topiary and its stonework. One was of a bow-legged old gardener standing beside a bed of delphiniums to demonstrate their height.

During her London fortnight, she went the rounds, and was envied. She lived in a busy whirl. As the others made their way in to dinner, she was always going in the opposite direction towards the swing doors, dressed in a long brocade dress with her fur coat over it and carrying a purse done in *petit-point* which Mrs Post had often gushingly admired. Summers had to spend a great deal of time out in the Cromwell Road, trying to get taxis for her.

In the mornings, she would hand round theatre programmes to the residents, or describe food, or drop names, as if sparing a few crumbs for the famished. 'You really *should* see it,' she told Mrs Arbuthnot. 'It's an absolute scream. Rather naughty, you know; but in a wholesome way, of course. One really *couldn't* take exception.' It was many years since Mrs Arbuthnot had seen a play, and she knew that she never would again.

'I fear my friends will kill me with kindness,' Lady Swayne told Mrs Palfrey. 'I suppose it's because I come for such a short stay, while *you* are in London all the time and the parties can be mercifully spread out. I must confess that I should sometimes like to let up a little, to have a nice quiet evening as you do; but, oh dear, no: no one will hear of it. "It will be another year before you come again," they say, "so we must make the most of you while you're here." *The Marjorie Swayne Festival*, Oscar Barrington jokingly called it. I expect you've heard of him. He's a famous critic on the *Sunday Times*.'

'No,' said Mrs Palfrey firmly. She had intended to be friendly, but began to feel that she had had enough. 'I take the *Observer*.'

'Do you!' Lady Swayne's light tone and the flicker of her eyelids seemed to say, 'Here's a queer fish indeed.' 'I'm afraid *we* gave *that* up at the time of Suez.'

That was another irritating mannerism – all of her most bigoted or self-congratulatory statements, she prefaced with 'I'm afraid'. I'm afraid I don't smoke. I'm afraid I'm just common-or-garden Church of England. (Someone had mentioned Brompton Oratory.) I'm afraid I'd like to see the Prime Minister hanged, drawn and quartered. I'm afraid I think the fox revels in it. I'm afraid I don't think that's awfully funny.

Some days after finding Mrs Palfrey's parcel outside his door, Ludo (having thought better about writing a note) turned up at the Claremont, wearing the very sweater, and having a bunch of violets in his hand. He was on his way home from work, and he had bought the flowers from a flower-stall, in Knightsbridge.

'Oh!' Mrs Palfrey breathed out, and she took the bunch in her trembling hands, and gazed at it. There were little drops of water among the violets to keep them from wilting, a cold, faint scent when she held the bunch to her nose. She sniffed – not prettily – but as if she were snuffing up something for her health's sake.

It was hanging-about hour in which – the menu already noted – one waited for dinner; Mrs Burton getting 'very-nicely-thank-you', as Mrs Arbuthnot put it, and Lady Swayne supposed by all to be putting on her brocade.

'Would you join me for dinner?' Mrs Palfrey asked Ludo. 'Oh, the sleeves are far too long. It's hopeless.'

'It's most beautifully warm, and I like it.'

'But will you?'

'I'm afraid I can't,' he said. She wondered if this were a sort of Lady Swayne parlance – the being afraid of what might positively please him. 'I'm expecting someone at home,' he added.

Mrs Palfrey was quite astonished, having imagined him living rather like a hermit, once back from Harrods, and writing, writing.

'A bird,' he said, and he narrowed his eyes mischievously, endearingly.

'A bird,' she murmured, giving herself time, and took another great sniff at the bunch of violets.

'Called Rosie.'

At that moment, out of the lift stepped brocaded Lady Swayne. Mrs Palfrey, who had sometimes in her life been majestic, but never graceful, thrust out the violets as Lady Swayne paused beside her.

'A breath of spring,' she said. She seemed uncoordinated, Ludo thought, like a robot that had gone wrong. Lady Swayne took full advantage of this state of mind, with a flowing, gracious gesture. 'Exquisite,' she breathed, in the softest of tones. 'Alas, though! They never last.'

'My grandson,' Mrs Palfrey continued wildly, nodding towards Ludo.

'Ah, I've heard of you; heard of you.'

'Desmond,' Mrs Palfrey added firmly. 'Lady Swayne.'

'You are at the B.M., I believe,' said Lady Swayne.

Mrs Palfrey was alarmed, but Ludo's pause was brief. 'For my sins,' he said, smiling. He had often thought of using this meaningless phrase, which was one of the Major's favourites.

'Do you know Carr Templeton?'

Mrs Palfrey was now mesmerised like a startled hare. 'Only vaguely,' said Ludo. He had quickly summed up Lady Swayne, and now decided that Carr Templeton must be grand, or would not have been mentioned by her. 'I am hardly on that plane as yet,' he said, and almost added 'for my sins' again, but took a grip of himself. He might have extricated himself by talking of being in different departments, if he had known what Carr Templeton's department was. He was not even sure of his own, and felt that the British Museum background should be gone into in greater detail.

'You are young,' Lady Swayne was saying graciously. 'Your time will come.'

'My Grandmamma is going to give me a glass of sherry.' ('For my sins' would have gone beautifully with that, too.) He moved a little, and took Mrs Palfrey's elbow.

'That will be nice,' said Lady Swayne. 'Your grandmother has such peaceful, quiet evenings that you will make a little change for her. Unlike poor little me.' (She was at least five feet ten, and with shoulders like a bison's.) 'I am whirled round London in a way more fitting to a deb than an old, old lady. Yes, a taxi, please, Summers. This evening ...' – she sighed – 'I'm off to the Savoy,' and then, to Ludo's immense delight, she added, 'for my sins.' It is infectious, he decided.

They left her to pace about while poor Summers kept leaping off the pavement outside, waving his arms, whistling shrilly into the twilight, to no avail.

Mrs Palfrey and Ludo went to the bar end of the lounge, the bell was pressed and Antonio, the ancient waiter, shuffled in. 'I always think Antonio is more the name for a *young* man,' Mrs Palfrey said in a low voice, having given her order. 'You came *so* well out of your ordeal, dear boy.'

She laid the violets carefully on the table. They were curling up already, Ludo noticed, as Lady Swayne so obviously had.

'I am sorry to enmesh you in this falsehood,' Mrs Palfrey said with dignity.

'Oh, I adore it,' he said. 'I love hazards, as long as they aren't the kind one can be put in prison for.'

'Oh, I should hope *not* – if I thought . . . '

'The Bristol Cream, the Tio Pepe,' Antonio said. His hands holding the tray shook – like most hands at the Claremont, Ludo supposed. *He* put his hands in his trousers, and tried, furtively, to reckon up how much money he had.

'Do let *me* pay for this,' he said, 'for I suggested it.'

'Certainly not,' said Mrs Palfrey. He had been sure she would. 'I am quite delighted to see you.'

'It was very kind of you,' he said, patting the sweater. 'I never had anything knitted especially for me before, except once my mother says she made me some leggings when I was little. When she sewed them up both feet faced the same way. No matter: I had to wear them. She crammed my little feet into them, and that's why I always walk like this now.' He got up and dragged his feet sideways across the carpet. Those same dangerous shoes, she noted.

'Oh, you'll be the death of me; you really will,' Mrs Palfrey said, laughing so much. She had not laughed for a long time.

Mrs Burton, sitting opposite them, threw back her head and laughed, too, wishing to join in the fun.

'Rather Bohemian,' Mrs Post, at the other end of the room, whispered behind her knitting to Mrs Arbuthnot.

Ludo came back to Mrs Palfrey, patted her hand and sat down beside her again.

He drank some sherry, and then murmured to her, 'I wonder about your friends here.'

She saw real concern on the face he turned towards her. 'Are they all that nice? Are they nice enough for *you*, I mean?'

That night she lay awake for a long time, savouring the phrase – *Are they nice enough for you, I mean?* She had had cherished things said to her in her life, but they were far away in the past. But such treasures, she thought, no one can ever take away.

Then, that girl, Rosie, the bird, she remembered. Is she still there? Like a frantic, left wife, she put on the light and looked at her watch. One-thirty. She smiled peacefully, the little flurry of pique over. She would have gone long ago. And next Saturday he had promised to come to me, she thought; and then at last she fell asleep.

9

Ludo sat in Harrods on a spring afternoon. The Exhibition Hall had been transformed into a garden with flower beds and bright green grass; fountains played and azaleas and carnations and lilies were all blooming together. Voices of people going round were muffled and wondering, they admired, bent to read labels and sniffed at roses. A record of birdsong was played. From beyond the lift hall, Ludo could hear it.

He sat on a squashy sofa beside one of the country women he knew so well from Harrods – up for the day, for Harley Street and shopping, and dog-tired.

He could not attend to his work. Soon it would be warm enough to stay at home all day. Although being in a crowd was distracting – especially so this afternoon for some reason – he was rather repelled by the thought of long, lonely hours behind his basement bars. Feet going by above him he would watch as if hypnotised, trying to imagine the rest of the bodies he could not see.

He now began to examine the legs of the woman sitting

next to him on the sofa – ginger lace-ups, wrinkled stockings, a neat crêpe bandage round one ankle. His eyes slyly travelled upwards. With a keen, sideways glance he quickly took in buttons of plaited leather on heather-mixture tweed, military-looking gloves.

None of this was of any use to him. He was simply wasting time and he knew it, and was filled with the dreadful despair of every writer who knows he is doing that. Not getting an armchair was to blame, he tried to believe. After he had come back from the Gents, his previous chair had been taken. Sometimes he had to hover about to get a chair at all, studying the incomprehensible Stock Exchange prices, sauntering up and down, waiting for one of the seated to be claimed by somebody, or feel rested enough to gather up parcels and go. Then he would pounce, as if playing musical chairs. He had become adept at guessing which person was likely to leave first.

He leaned back and shut his eyes. Typewriting could be heard – a spasmodic clacking. Above the sound of birdsong, the lift ladies chirrupped 'Going up', in their refined voices.

He stole another sideways look. The woman had a silver-mounted eagle's claw pinned to her lapel. It was difficult to let his eyes travel higher than this, without staring into her face, meeting her eyes, perhaps. Presently, he shifted his position, cleared his throat and took a quick glance at her, as if looking expectantly beyond her for someone to emerge from a lift. Beret of brown crocheted wool. She turned her head. Pebble spectacles, he noted, and looked away, at the clock, to emphasise his mood of expectancy, of impatience, even.

As if tired of being studied, the woman sighed and stirred

and collected herself, got up and walked away, dragging one foot a little. Pepper and salt hair.

He wrote down *Pepper-and-salt hair*, so that he should be writing something. Then began to look about him again, at people passing to and fro, or sitting near by. *Physiognomy*, he wrote above *Pepper-and-salt hair*, and underlined it. From time to time he added to a list as if he really were making a serious study. *Cleft chin, widow's peak, Hapsburg lip* and *five o'clock shadow*. By simply rearranging these words he could later make a poem out of them, he decided. He knew nothing about poetry, apart from assistant-stage-managing *The Cocktail Party* when he was in the repertory company. *Dowager's hump*, he wrote. *Port-wine nose, wasp-waist*, and *club-foot*. He ceased to look about him, and continued the game from inside his mind with *pony tail, crow's-feet* and *cauliflower ears, hang-nails* and *hammer-toes* and *fallen arches. Pursed lips, parched lips, eye-teeth, dog-teeth, wisdom-teeth, buck-teeth. Bone-idle.* Brought up by the oddness of this, he paused. What on earth did *bone-idle* mean? He frowned. '*Wall-eyed*', he quickly scribbled, suddenly seeing someone with this affliction.

'I have brought you a steak and kidney pie,' Mrs Palfrey said, standing before him.

In hasty confusion, as if he were a schoolboy found reading something pornographic, he hid his writing behind his back, and rose.

'A steak and kidney pie?' he asked.

'I glimpsed you there as I went through to the Food Hall to buy some Garibaldi biscuits. I often nibble a biscuit in the night if I can't sleep. Then I went to look at the wedding-cakes – such a sign of spring, I always feel. I love to see them –

and they were just bringing in a fresh lot of pies. "Just the thing for Desmond's supper," I thought. It's still warm, in fact; but you'll need to put it in the oven for a while.' She held out her parcel for him to take it, her eyes bright with pleasure. *Dancing eyes*, he thought, as if he were now possessed of a tic.

'Do sit down,' he said, indicating with the pie the place beside him.

'Oh, no, I mustn't interrupt your work,' she said firmly.

There was no sarcasm in her voice. After all, she could not know what he had been writing.

'I have come to a block,' he said. 'Please sit and chat me up for a moment.'

She sat down and settled herself, and smiled.

'You are too kind to me,' he said, looking at the pie. He sat down beside her, holding it carefully on his knees, the pages of writing now stuffed into his pocket.

'You have been kind to me,' she said, 'on more than one occasion.'

'Well, it will be such a treat. I don't know when I last had one of these. Pies, I mean. Why don't you come along this evening and share it with me?' (What am I *saying*? he wondered. He seemed to have no power over himself this day.) 'I've been so stuck with my writing I need company.' The evening was wasted from the start, with Rosie at her Judo class.

Mrs Palfrey blushed.

'I couldn't do that,' she said.

'I can't think why not. Surely a pie like this is big enough for two?'

'You can hardly want an old woman's company.'

'As for that, people's ages mean nothing to me,' Ludo said airily, secure in his youth. 'And it was my idea,' he added.

Mrs Palfrey now looked flustered, clearly having in her mind accepted his invitation. 'Then I shall go off again and forage for some cheese. Oh, it will be such a chance,' she said warmly. 'I always look at the cheese and wish I had an occasion to buy some. One misses one's housekeeping and shopping. I shall go on my own,' she insisted, as he looked as if he were about to accompany her. She now had a mind to buy other things as well – Bath Olivers and chocolate mints, and whatever else might take her fancy.

'Is there any kind of cheese you prefer?' she asked.

'I like all kinds. I leave it to you. But I insist on paying for it.'

'I have a Harrods' card,' Mrs Palfrey said, as if, because of this, money was not involved.

'There is a tin of beans at home,' Ludo said, trying to contribute something to the feast.

'Splendid!' Mrs Palfrey said, setting off, walking so much better now that spring had come.

Ludo leaned back, watching her, wondering about the evening before him. The warmth from the pie he held was comforting. He hoped it wasn't going to slop about. He could faintly smell it through its wrappings, and felt hungry.

Mrs Palfrey returned with a carrier-bag with 'Harrods' printed on it. She set it down carefully beside him and said, 'You could bring your sandwiches and your writing things in that. It would make you look more authentic. As a shopper, I mean.'

'You think of everything.'

Mrs Palfrey thought, I do where you're concerned, my dear Desmond. I try to go one step ahead of you, to discover what you want. She felt suddenly tired, from love. A cup of tea and a little lie-down on returning to the Claremont would set her right, she decided, and then she would change into her maroon wool and parade herself a little before the other ladies. 'I shan't be in to dinner,' she would say.

'I hope you can manage to carry it all,' she said to Ludo. 'For I am sure that I couldn't. The pie could balance on the top of the rest.'

'No problem. I have the strength. Why, I could lift *you* up in my arms just as if you were a little baby,' he said in – for some reason – an Irish accent. A woman sitting in the chair next to him turned sharply. Mrs Palfrey and Ludo, at this, looked steadily at one another, suppressing laughter.

'What time?' she then whispered, like a girl.

'Seven-thirty for eight,' he whispered back.

She stumped off to the front entrance to put herself in the care of the commissionaire for a taxi. She was spending money recklessly today; but it's only once in a while, she told herself, making her way through Jewelry and Gloves.

'Seven-thirty for eight.' She smiled. Oh, he's a funny boy. She wished that she had had a son. But he'd be old now. Her grandson? There was always Desmond, the real Desmond. She shrugged. Someone held open the great glass door for her. There never *was* Desmond, and thank heaven for that.

'Good-bye, madam. Thank you. So nice to see you again. Keep well,' said the commissionaire, palming her sixpence, smiling and nodding. She always gave sixpence. Always had.

*

The spring evening was beautiful. It was keeping light so late, people said. They were drawing out, the days. Behind the budding lilacs in the Square, huge cumulus clouds reflected the setting sun, looking like a range of the Alps. Mrs Palfrey, half-closing her eyes, could imagine them as snow. Doing so, she veered a little across the pavement, then pulled herself together. She was so full of happiness, even though nobody had been about in the vestibule to see her leave. No matter: she would be missed at dinner.

Starlings, gathering to roost on the ledges of buildings, were making a commotion above her. At a street corner, a man was wheeling away a barrow of daffodils and irises, and the barrow was draped with artificial grass so much more brilliant than the sad stuff in the gardens of the Square. Little dogs were being taken for their evening walks, and people strolled along, looking through the railings at budding shrubs, noticing things about them as if for the first time this year.

As she carefully descended the area steps, Mrs Palfrey could see Ludo in the lighted room, putting something on the table.

He opened the door to her and took her coat and complimented her upon her string of pearls, as if he could not think of anything else to say. To her disappointment, there was suddenly an air of constraint between them. She touched the pearls from nervousness, went over to the gas-fire and chafed her hands, though she was not cold. He watched her. Veins the colour of pewter branched over the back of those transparent hands. He took in every detail of her while she bent there before the fire – her heavy rings, the neatly-pleated handkerchief tucked in her cuff, folds of skin about her jowl, hanging loose. She had taken age as it came, and it had come apace.

She felt him looking at her, and straightened her back, with a creaking, uneasy sound, like an old tree in a high wind. His gaze at once slithered away, and he began to touch things on the table, rearranging what he had already set out – plates (there was nowhere to warm them, she realised, save on the floor before the gas-fire), odd knives and forks, two Kleenex tissues for napkins. He had gone to some thought and trouble; had perhaps become a little fussed. There was also a half bottle of Mateus Rosé; one glass, and a yoghourt carton in place of the second.

'There was no time to get the silver from the bank,' he said, standing back and surveying the table.

'This is fun for me,' she said. But is it? she wondered. Having said the words, she dared not dwell on them.

The pie was warming – but never would right through – on an asbestos mat above the gas-fire. Mrs Palfrey, having imagined an oven, now saw that the pie was an embarrassment. And she had put him to the expense of the wine, so really it was *she* who was the embarrassment.

He moved away from the table and she went to the window and looked up at the darkening street. No one passed.

'I am afraid it is Cyprus – Cypriot,' he said, handing her a little glass with '*Olé*' painted on it. 'Not like your usual Bristol Cream.'

Oh, sherry, too! Mrs Palfrey thought, feeling drowned in shame.

'Mine has "*Sköl*" on it,' Ludo said, raising his glass. 'They were thrown in with the rest of the furniture, and I find them quite charming. "*Salute*", got broken. To your good health, Mrs Palfrey, Grandmamma!'

'Oh, to yours!' she said.

'Is it too horrible?' he asked anxiously.

'It is quite delicious,' she replied, then, cancelling the validity of that, added, 'I don't know one kind of sherry from another.'

'I sometimes wonder what sort of person lived here before, and bought them – the glasses – and left them. They would hardly be provided by the landlord, would they? *Things* don't matter much to me; or, rather, awful or beautiful, they seem to interest me the same.'

'Because you are a writer,' Mrs Palfrey said solemnly, and her colour rose slightly, as if she had touched on something sacred.

There had never been anyone like her in Ludo's life – no spoiling aunt, or comfortable Nannie, no doting elder sisters – just he and his mother living in too close quarters, and quarrelling. No one that he knew stood in awe of writers. The Major had told him one day that in five years' time no one would read any more. Later, archaeologists would ponder on, argue about, what books had been *for*. 'It'll all be telly; visual aids.' 'Then why are more books published every year?' Ludo had asked, annoyed with him as usual. 'Show me the figures, laddie. Show me the figures.'

'Why do you look so annoyed?' Mrs Palfrey asked him. 'I shall think it is *you* who doesn't like the sherry.'

'I adore the sherry. But someone I *don't* adore passed through my mind. My mother's lover – the Major.'

As if in a panic, he brought the half-bottle of Aphrodite Medium-Dry, and refilled her glass.

'Goodness, if I drink all this I'll have to have a cab to take me home.'

'Well, we arranged it once before.'

'What a strange friendship we have,' she murmured, and looked away with a clumsy movement.

Ludo thought of the man, her husband, who had had to woo her in those far-off days, and wondered at his courage. The spirit of the Empire-builders. He'd gone battling on, undaunted, and got someone brave and staunch. Not a bad thing to have.

The sherry had broken the ice, as he had hoped it would.

The supper was a success of a kind.

When he had made some coffee, Ludo read a quiz from an evening paper he had picked up from a chair in Harrods. He asked her questions, looking across at her, with pencil ready for a tick or a cross, his eyebrows raised inquiringly.

'Do you prefer to be a host or a guest?'

She could think of the question only in terms of him. 'Well, I loved that evening when you came to dinner at the Claremont; but I must confess I have preferred being here,' she said.

'If you were kept waiting by a friend you had arranged to meet, would you (a) wait patiently and be forgiving when he or she arrived, so that you could both in the end enjoy the evening, (b) go on waiting, and have a row when whoever it is turns up, or (c) go home?'

Seriously, she pondered the question, trying to give a true reply.

'Have a chocolate mint,' he said, pushing the box across the table.

She took one, but, before putting it in her mouth, said, 'I know you wouldn't keep me waiting, except for a very good reason. I should wait patiently, so that we might both enjoy the rest of the evening.'

'No, not just *me*,' he said. 'Anyone.'

'There *is* no one,' she said. 'I can't think of anyone else.'

He blinked his eyes, and then went on in a matter-of-fact way.

'Do you ever break your word?'

'No,' she said at once.

'Do you consider yourself an optimistic person?'

'Oh, I think so.' She did not explain to him how deeply pessimistic one must be in the first place, to need the sort of optimism she now had at her command.

'Would you rush to get a hair appointment before an unexpected invitation?' he asked, in a rather low, reluctant voice.

Cheerfully, she said, 'I go to the hairdresser every other Friday.'

He began to add up her score, and she sat thinking.

'You have an average capacity for friendship,' he announced.

'I shouldn't have thought so,' she said, smiling. 'Not after what I just had to confess. Of course, I found it easier to make friends when Arthur was alive – other couples, you know. We dined at one another's houses. Widows aren't quite the same thing: they get asked only to large parties where odd numbers don't matter, and are really only seldom asked to *them*. And then, as one gets older, people die, or drop out of one's life for other reasons. One is left with very little. Shall I ask *you* the questions now?'

'No, I know the way the answers have to go. I think my result would have been much the same as yours.'

In a rather dreamy voice, Mrs Palfrey went on, 'Sometimes, when I was a young, married woman, I longed to be freed – free of nursery chores and social obligations, one's duty, d'you know? And free of worries, too, about one's loved ones – childish ailments and ageing parents, money troubles, everyone at times feels the longing – to run away from it all. But it's really not to be desired – and I realise that that's the only *way* of being free – to be not needed.' He seemed as if he were going to interrupt her, but she went smoothly on, turning the rings on her fingers, looking across at the fire. 'My daughter no longer needs me – indeed, her dread is that it might one day be the other way about. You've seen how much Desmond needs me. And there's no one I know who could ever be a burden to me now.'

'In a way,' Ludo began, hoping to remember some of the conversation for future use, 'in a way, I need you.'

She blushed a little, looked flustered, and laughed. 'I don't think so,' she said, in ignorance, naturally, of what he meant.

'I haven't many friends myself,' he said, looking surprised at this realisation. 'One needs money to have friends. They've all got cars and jobs – the ones I used to know.'

'One shouldn't let one's friends slip away.'

'Not much I can do about it.'

'What *do* you live on?' she asked gently, feeling that from her great age she could.

'Very little. I have some money from my grandmother. My *other* grandmother,' he said. 'My *dead* grandmother. You are my third and only living grandmother.'

I shall leave him a little, too, for a surprise, Mrs Palfrey decided. She thought about dying more and more as the months went by, yet dreaded it less. She could make her arrangements without sadness and panic.

'You're young,' she said. 'It doesn't matter so much. But it's nice to be comfortably placed when one is older. To be able to afford the Claremont, instead of living alone in one room.'

For the first time, he saw that one might live long enough to be grateful for the Claremont.

'Rosie,' Mrs Palfrey said, rather hesitantly. 'Now, there's a friend you have – for you told me so yourself.'

'I really hardly know her,' Ludo said (except in the Biblical sense, he added, to himself.)

'Shall we wash up now?' she suggested.

'No, I shall do it later.'

'Then I think I should be getting back.'

'I'll go and look for a taxi.'

'No, my dear. The walk will be good for me.'

'Then I shall come with you, and it can be good for me, too.'

'My nicest evening, I think, since Arthur died,' she said, as he helped her into her coat.

He opened the door into the area. A fine drizzle was falling without sound upon the dustbin lids and railings, and he fetched a rather broken umbrella, another relic from a former occupier.

'It's nothing much,' he said, meaning the rain.

He took her arm, and guided her along the wet pavement, holding the umbrella over her and, under it, giving her little sidelong glances, as young people do the old, as if they wonder if they will collapse or crumble away at any moment.

A fresh cold smell came from the gardens – the rain on the

sour grass, damping the grit and seeds blown down the paths, and the sharpness of all the new small leaves.

He saw her right up the steps and into the Claremont. She made quite a little stir, saying 'good night' and 'thank you' to him, and showing off rather like a child. The manager, happening to be there, greeted her cordially: Mrs Post stood waiting for the lift, after her dull evening, rolled-up knitting under her arm; and Mr Osmond was showing a captive American one-night guest the clipping of his letter to the *Evening News*.

It was a splendid entrance Mrs Palfrey was able to make. Ludo, guessing this, blew her a kiss as he went back through the revolving doors.

In bliss she went to bed.

Ludo hurried back home to write up his notes.

10

Full summer; and Mrs Arbuthnot left the Claremont. It was going downhill, she said. Trippery people coming at random. It was not the place she had once known. 'We used to have bridge,' she said wistfully. 'A dowager countess stayed here.' In truth, Mrs Arbuthnot had become incontinent, and in the nicest possible way, which in the circumstances could not be very nice, had been asked to make some other arrangement.

She was vague about her destination, mentioning a quiet hotel on the outskirts of London, which was in reality a nursing-home for elderly people, where she was to share a small bedroom, and so finish up her days. Her indefatigable sisters had found it for her, and much humiliation she had borne while they were doing so.

'Shall have some peace at least,' she said, surveying the Cromwell Road traffic from one of the chairs at the top of the steps, waiting for her sisters to fetch her. Her cases stood in the vestibule. She had tears in her eyes.

'May I visit you there?' Mrs Palfrey asked on an impulse. She had come out to say good-bye, and help if she could.

Mrs Arbuthnot turned stiffly, but looked at Mrs Palfrey's feet and not her face. 'I can't think that either of us would gain from that,' she said.

She was filled with agony, and she spat it out where she could. What she had been through, no one should ever know – those middle-of-the-night dreams of relieving herself, of finding after long searching a Ladies' room in some mazy hotel – oh, the release of it! Only to wake up and find the bed saturated, and herself stiff and helpless. It could not go on, she knew. It had happened three times. A kind Irish chambermaid had tried to cover up for her; but the housekeeper found out in the end. Now someone must be paid to dry up after her; soon, not only that, but put on her shoes, get her up from her chair.

Mrs Post paused on her way out. She was wearing, in spite of the warm afternoon, her mock (and as far as Mrs Arbuthnot was concerned, her mocked *at*) fur coat of grey shaded stripes. If I were going to copy any kind of fur, Mrs Arbuthnot thought, consoling herself, it would not be squirrel.

'Do let me have your address,' said Mrs Post. 'I can write you a newsy little letter now and again about all the goings-on here.' She made the Claremont seem the very hub of life.

'I will send it to you,' Mrs Arbuthnot said. 'If I find the hotel to my liking – enough to stay there, that is.' She would never see or hear anything from any of them again. Her mind was made up to that.

Mrs Palfrey, still looking stern from the rudeness she had suffered, said good-bye in a formal voice and went back inside to write a letter to her daughter. There was an indefinable melancholy about Mrs Arbuthnot's departure. Mrs Palfrey began to wonder if they had been given the true reasons – if the move were not an enforced one for the sake of economy.

She sat down at the writing-table. There was only one sheet of Claremont paper in the drawer. The printed sheets were always rather pounced upon, and Mr Osmond was the worst culprit.

'Dear Elizabeth,' wrote Mrs Palfrey. She took her daughter's latest letter from her handbag and re-read it, with pursed lips. It was about the bottling of gooseberries and the weights of salmon, about neighbours her mother had never met, and Scottish orgies she could not imagine. Up there, they were for ever coming home in the wee sma' hours. Of course, they were known for their hardiness, Mrs Palfrey knew, and the farther south one comes the more that disappears; but Elizabeth and Ian were not young, and Elizabeth had been born in Tunbridge Wells, which could avail her nothing. She was not bred to Hogmanay, or dancing reels, or going out with the guns, but she had surrendered herself to it as if it were all she could ever have desired. Mrs Palfrey found this a strange reaction to a foreign country. For her part, only when she had been abroad, had she consciously thought, 'I am English'. She had kept *that* barrier up, she proudly remembered now, pondering instead of writing. It had been her solace for homesickness, her defiance from fear, her affirmation of her origins. When she was young, it had seemed that nearly all the world was pink on her school atlas – 'ours', in fact. Nearly all ours! she had thought. Pink was the colour, and the word, of well-being, and of optimism. To be born into it was the greatest luck. 'I am in the pink. So glad to know you've settled in,' had concluded her letter. As if I had just started at boarding-school, thought Mrs Palfrey. And it would have been her second term by now.

'Thank you for your letter,' she wrote. She paused. 'I was interested to hear . . .'

There was a little commotion on the front steps and she went to one of the windows which looked down on them. She parted the net curtains slightly, as if watching a funeral go by. Mrs Arbuthnot was being helped down the steps and into an ancient Daimler.

I shall never see her again, Mrs Palfrey thought. There was nothing more to fear from that sharp tongue. Into the afternoon traffic Mrs Arbuthnot was driven away. She did not turn her head to see Mrs Post, standing at the top of the steps waving a handkerchief.

Summers, the hall porter, pocketing a florin, came back up the steps; and presently Mrs Post descended them, feeling suddenly at a loss, with no more errands to run for Mrs Arbuthnot.

'. . . that Desmond has been visiting you,' Mrs Palfrey, sitting down again, added to her letter. 'It was nice that he could spare the time from his work.' Rather catty, she thought; but let it go.

After all these years there was no communication with her only child. These letters between them were either a farce or a formality.

Mr Osmond came in and looked annoyed at the sight of Mrs Palfrey sitting at the only writing-desk. He took up a magazine and fidgeted about.

'Our company is sadly depleted,' he observed.

'Yes, indeed,' Mrs Palfrey agreed, looking up.

'The so-called hotel is, in fact, a nursing-home, you know.'
'Which so-called hotel?'

'The one to which Mrs Arbuthnot has repaired. A nursing-home not of the first order, moreover. They will let her die there: as she deteriorates, they will not be bothered to get her out of bed.'

'If this is true, we can be sure that Mrs Arbuthnot did not want us to know it,' Mrs Palfrey said, in what Mr Osmond considered a priggish tone.

'It *is* true,' he said.

'Did Mrs Arbuthnot herself tell you?'

'No. Summers mentioned a forwarding address. It so happens that an old cousin of mine died there – at the Braemar. I visited her once or twice. I was not impressed by it. My wife . . . ' He had been going to speak of the superior nursing-home where *she* had died, but he could not go on. His face collapsed. He put his fingers to his moustache, then cast a glance inside his magazine.

'Poor Mrs Arbuthnot! She must have been in far worse shape than one imagined,' Mrs Palfrey said, feeling upset. So readily she forgave that earlier rudeness, everything.

Mr Osmond now looked pointedly at the letter she was writing, feeling it was time she put an end to it. 'I'm sorry to have interrupted you,' he said.

Mrs Palfrey bent her head, but she could not concentrate on her task with Mr Osmond hovering about. She wrote a little more – praised the weather, sent her kind regards to Ian – and finished – 'Loving Mother'.

As she addressed the envelope, Mr Osmond watched her anxiously, hoping she would not begin another letter. But no, she stamped it and then rose. She would post it after tea, she said, amused by his impatience. As soon as the door closed after her, he hurried to the desk and opened the drawer. It was empty except for an old piece of blotting-paper. He slammed the drawer shut in great vexation, and strode off to the reception-desk, with 'Dear Sir' boiling in his mind, the beginnings of his letter half composed already – a furious complaint to the Postmaster-General, about delays in mail deliveries, with instances and dates. The receptionist, under directions from the manager, handed him one sheet of paper, one envelope, taking them slowly from the stationery cupboard on which she then firmly turned the key.

Mrs Palfrey, having posted her letter, walked for a little longer in the dusty summer streets, and away from the rush-hour traffic. Her life at the Claremont was so much more endurable in this warmer weather, her time more easily filled. She had almost a sense of freedom. But this evening, Mrs Arbuthnot's departure had cast a shadow. Mrs Palfrey could not help referring the situation to herself, imagining herself immobile in the inferior nursing-home. Must keep going, she thought, as she so often thought. Every day for years she had memorised a few lines of poetry to train her mind against threatening forgetfulness. She now determined to train her limbs against similar uselessness. Although tired, she went on past her usual turning-place, thought she would stroll down Ludo's street, and so make the round journey.

The world is too much with us; late and soon,
Getting and spending, we lay waste our powers.

Her lips moved gently as she tried to remember her lines for the day. By tomorrow she would have forgotten them. Only the poetry she had learned by heart as a girl remained.

Little we see in Nature that is ours;

She was stuck after the third line. That was the way it went with her these days.

Ludo was home already. Down in that dark basement she saw him pass across, wearing the sweater she had knitted for him. She would not dream of calling, but she stood by the railings for a moment and waved.

Instead of Ludo, a girl wearing his sweater, came to the window and stood looking up, holding back the curtains on either side of her.

Mrs Palfrey nodded curtly and walked on. She felt in a commotion and could not sort out what she was feeling, only knowing that she had made a fool of herself. To her, there was something intimate about wearing other people's clothes. She brushed that thought aside, feeling breathless with jealousy. She wished that she had taken another direction. Now she would feel put out all the evening. She veered across the pavement in her agitation. Cucumber sandwiches she had had for tea repeated.

'Some old girl standing there waving,' Rosie said.

'Mrs Palfrey,' Ludo said, when she had been described. 'You know, I've told you. Wanting a chat perhaps.'

He had been out to Putney to see his mother, who was lying in bed with what she called 'summer' flu'. The room had been stuffy and Ludo had kept looking at the clock. She was tousled and blotchy. The bed was strewn with screwed-up tissues and discarded hot water bottles. On the bedside table were sticky bottles and smeared glasses and a plate with some egg on it. The Major had given her a gin-and-french and a bite to eat, and gone back to work. Ludo had sat on the bed reading Woman's Own for half an hour, had filled a hot water bottle, fetched another gin-and-french, and felt that he had done his duty. While waiting for the kettle to boil, he had explored the food cupboard and spread some peanut butter on a crust of new bread and eaten it quickly. Cheese on a plate had a green fuzz half an inch high.

'It's a strange set-up,' he told Rosie. 'No husband would stand for it. So why he, who doesn't have to?'

'There's no accounting for tastes. Perhaps she's unusual in bed.'

Ludo felt such distaste that he changed the subject. 'Why my sweater?' he asked.

'Because it's so chilly down here. It's like the bowels of the earth. I've done the salad.'

'Stout work, as the Major would say.'

Leaving his mother's flat he had met the Major by the front door, coming early from his office to show his devotion. He was wearing a crumpled light-weight suit of a pale colour and a tie with a pattern of tankards on it. He carried a wrapped-up bottle.

'How's tricks, old fellow? Full of the joys?'

They had talked a little about what he called 'our invalid', then he had told what Ludo considered a perfectly filthy story, and gone stumping upstairs to the love-nest.

'You see this egg,' Ludo now said to Rosie, and held one up, about to make an omelette. 'Would you believe that if I hold it end to end like this between the palms of my hands and squeeze hard it won't break?'

'No I wouldn't.'

'And squeeze ... and squeeze ...' The egg broke and yolk ran down his trousers.

Rosie stared at him.

'Well, I'm damned, that's never happened before. It's supposed to be impossible.'

'You must be going out of your mind.'

'I swear I've done it hundreds of times. God, what a mess.'

She fetched a damp cloth and began to clean his trousers, kneeling before him, looking cross. He stared down fondly at her dusty-looking hair, still dyed grey as when he had met her first, although she often talked of making a change.

'Well, we shall just have to have a smaller omelette than I'd meant,' he said cheerfully.

The major shouted out from the kitchen, 'Did you have that nice crust of bread?'

'Don't be a fool.'

'Well, it's gone. That bloody boy, I s'pose.'

'My son, you mean.'

But they weren't really quarrelling. They never did.

'I'd looked forward to that,' the Major said, covering his disappointment with a jolly laugh.

11

Mrs de Salis was all that Mrs Post could have wished for – a confidante, a companion, a diversion, a chatterbox. She arrived at the Claremont from a convalescence in a nursing-home, and brought stories of doctors and operations, of tiffs and feuds, of wrong diagnoses and medical neglect. In fact, she hardly stopped talking except at meal-times, when she sat at Mrs Arbuthnot's old table and ate in what appeared to be an appalled silence.

She might have felt set apart from the others by her youth-fulness (she was only sixty), and the fact that she was a bird of passage as she put it, was looking for a flat in London – Cheyne Walk, she stipulated; or Little Venice.

'I love to look out over water,' she declared, looking out over the Cromwell Road.

'Difficult, I'd think, to discover anything in those areas,' Mrs Post said, hoping that it would, in fact, be found to be impossible. 'So sought after.' So expensive, she added to herself.

'I've never been beaten yet,' said Mrs de Salis.

She had a low, husky voice, rather actressy, Mrs Post thought. The general effect of her was fashionable. She made that impression, in spite of being rather careless – scarves tied anyhow and dresses hanging below coats, a button missing that never was to be replaced.

On the summer evenings after dinner they sat together, a thing they had not done before – Mrs Palfrey, Mrs Burton, with a drink beside her, Mrs Post always next to Mrs de Salis, Mr Osmond not of, but near, the group. The armchairs were pushed about – a thing the manager did not like.

'Have you any children?' Mrs Post asked Mrs de Salis.

'I have my beautiful Willie.'

Mrs de Salis brought out from her vast handbag a photograph of a young and pretty man, with drowsy eyes and dimpled chin. The ladies exclaimed over his looks. Mr Osmond gave one glance at the photograph and handed it back in silence, with a curious expression on his face.

'I *dote* on him,' said Mrs de Salis. 'I adore my darling Willie.'

'Shall we see him?' Mrs Post asked breathlessly.

'I shouldn't think so for a moment,' Mrs de Salis said gaily, thus knocking down all the structure of face-saving, of pretence, that had gone on for ever at the Claremont. 'Willie's got other fish to fry.'

I wish I'd thought of saying that about Desmond, Mrs Palfrey decided. *That* was the thing to say, saving all subterfuge. I could have overridden the shame, if *she* can.

'Oh, what a pity!' Mrs Post said, but only pitying *herself* for missing that extra excitement. 'It would have been nice.'

'I can't imagine Willie at the Claremont,' said Mrs de

Salis and, as none of them could either, no one took offence.

'Some young people *do* come,' Mrs Burton said. 'For instance, Mrs Palfrey's grandson. He's quite gorgeous, too.'

'Have you a photograph?' asked Mrs de Salis.

'Not on me,' Mrs Palfrey said.

'Well, I carry my adorable Willie with me wherever I go. He's so *special* to me – perhaps *extra* special because I had such a terrible time when he was born. They say those things fade from one's mind, but it never will from mine.'

Mr Osmond laced his fingers across his chest, leaned back and closed his eyes, making it clear that he was unable to concentrate on his crossword.

'It wasn't on the cards that I should live,' Mrs de Salis continued. 'They did a Caesar in the end.'

Mrs Palfrey began to disapprove. She even looked vaguely at the back page of the *Daily Telegraph* which, she, too, had folded for the crossword.

'What do you make of five down?' Mr Osmond called across, as if to a kindred soul. 'I can't finish it today. I think they've got a different fellow setting it. Can't get his drift. Our usual one on holiday, I shouldn't wonder.'

Mrs Palfrey pondered. 'Isn't it "nomadic"?' she asked in a modest tone.

'My goodness, I believe you're right.'

Mrs Burton was now in full swing. 'When I have my operations I always tell the anaesthetist ... quite frankly ... I tell them ... well, doesn't it make sense? ... I drink a lot, I say. I smoke a lot. I drink a lot. So I need more than most people to put me out. The pre-med's not working, I'll say ...'

She was rather forcing Mrs de Salis downstage. They both began to talk at once.

'. . . it was dehydration . . .'

'. . . I have no wish for waking up on the table, I said . . .'

'. . . tubes up my nose . . .' cried Mrs de Salis.

'Did you enjoy your dinner, Mrs Palfrey?' Mr Osmond asked – he hoped pointedly – across them.

'Well, I *do* think that green pea soup is my favourite.'

'They're very good with their *croûtons* here.'

'I had an operation once,' Mrs Post dared to say.

'Only *one!*' said Mrs de Salis. I wish I could look back and say the same. Was it major?' She glanced at Mr Osmond. 'Or mustn't one inquire?'

'Well, I don't suppose it was major,' Mrs Post said sadly. 'I broke my nose, and had to have it straightened.'

'Ah, yes,' Mrs de Salis said dismissingly. 'I suppose you just had a local anaesthetic'

'No, we were living in Norfolk at the time, and my husband insisted on my coming to London.'

'I didn't mean that,' Mrs de Salis said, and had a trilling laugh ready to follow. 'Have you had any operations, Mrs Palfrey?' she asked politely.

'No, and don't wish to have any,' Mrs Palfrey said to an astonished audience.

Mrs Burton, in the slight pause that followed, walked across the room and pressed the bell for the waiter.

'I thought the chicken wasn't half bad,' said Mr Osmond.

'There is so much chicken nowadays,' Mrs Palfrey complained. 'Once it was a treat.'

'Oh, I agree there.'

ELIZABETH TAYLOR

'Variety becomes more and more important as one gets older. There don't seem to be enough animals and birds.'

'Yes, lamb on Sunday, and it's round again in three. I agree with you. Only three animals, really.'

'Of course, there's veal, but . . . '

'Veal's expensive. I was looking at veal yesterday in Harrods.'

'Oh, do *you* go to Harrods?' Mrs Palfrey asked in great alarm.

'I think the butchery department is one of the sights of London – and those marble beds for the fish to lie in state on! Why, I'd rather go there than the National Gallery. The way they arrange their scallops and suchlike.'

'Twenty-one stitches,' said Mrs de Salis in her carrying voice.

'Of course, there's turkey at Christmas,' Mr Osmond reminded them. 'They do us quite well at Christmas.'

'I haven't had a Christmas here,' said Mrs Palfrey.

'Christmas is quiet,' said Mrs Post.

'Christmas is sad,' said Mr Osmond, almost to himself.

'They feel they must do something about it, d'you see; but they wish that we weren't here,' Mrs Post said. 'Sometimes one *hasn't* been; but it isn't always convenient at that time of the year to go away, to relations and so on; travelling is *so* risky.'

Mrs Palfrey felt foreboding.

'One or two local people come in – to the actual Christmas dinner,' Mrs Post went on. 'From those flats in the Square, I expect. Can't be bothered to cook for themselves, I suppose, and I can't blame them. We have turkey and all the trimmings, and they put up some decorations.'

'The same old decorations,' Mrs Burton said.

'And there's a little tree in the hall. I'm always glad when it's over,' Mrs Post said in an exhausted voice, as if she had just survived the ordeal.

'It doesn't sound very festive,' said Mrs de Salis. 'You'll all have to come to me in Cheyne Walk or wherever. I'll give a party.'

At this unusual word, Mr Osmond looked up, startled.

'Yes, you, too, darling,' Mrs de Salis said, meeting his glance.

Oh, how wistfully Mrs Post dwelt on the idea! It will never happen, she thought sadly. Once she's gone away, she'll quite forget.

Mr Osmond, flushed, returned to his crossword puzzle.

'It's that bloody motor show I hate,' said Mrs Burton, now well on, and with another drink beside her. '*That's* when they'd like us elsewhere. Mr Wilkins going on and on about how he could sell each room ten times over. Not a bed to be found in London for love or money, that's his theme-song. I get fed up with hearing him telling us.'

'Yes, we feel quite *de trop*,' said Mrs Post.

'I like Mr Wilkins's nerve,' said Mrs de Salis, meaning that she did not. 'We are paying dearly for what we get, I should have thought.' She spoke as if in the role of their leader. This was outspoken talk; for how much was paid, by whom, was a matter for reticence.

'But *reduced*,' Mrs Post said in a timid voice, 'it is *reduced*.'

'For obvious reasons,' said Mr Osmond.

At that moment, the receptionist looked in, cast a glance of disapproval at the rearranged chairs, and said to Mrs Palfrey,

'There is a young gentleman in the vestibule would like to see you.'

Mrs Palfrey got up, rather flustered.

'Your grandson, sure to be,' Mrs Post said, quite excitedly.

Standing in the vestibule, reading notices about Church Services, was not Ludo, as Mrs Palfrey had expected, but Desmond, the real Desmond.

He turned and looked at her coolly through thick spectacles which magnified his pale grey eyes.

Mrs Palfrey glanced about her. The hall, for that moment, was empty.

She went to him and gave his cheek a peck.

'You can't come here,' she hissed.

'But mother said I had to,' he replied.

12

Mrs Palfrey and *le vrai* Desmond walked round the Square. She had almost hustled him from the Claremont.

'It isn't done, do you see?' she said. 'To have visitors, I mean. For one thing, there is nowhere to entertain them, except in the lounge where one would disturb some very old people who like to be quiet, or in the television room where one would be disturbing the television. And at *this* time, Desmond! Why, it was getting on for nine o'clock.'

'One has one's work to do. I am writing a book.'

Oh, not another one, she thought. She seemed surrounded by authors.

'On Cycladic art,' he added.

'Well, I am sure your mother will be very proud of you,' Mrs Palfrey said, and then – it was so on her mind – 'So it would be better if you don't come again, you understand.'

'But once you wrote and asked me to dinner,' he protested.

'That was before I understood the – the position,' Mrs Palfrey said firmly.

'It isn't a *prison* you've found for yourself, is it?' he asked, really annoyed. 'Or a lunatic asylum?' He was furious with his mother for insisting on this absurd meeting. 'Pop in just once. That's all I ask,' she had written.

'You're more than welcome to dine with me at any time,' Mrs Palfrey said. 'Anywhere of your choosing,' she added recklessly. 'Apart from everything else, I should be ashamed to offer you the Claremont food.'

'It has gone downhill since you first suggested it?' Desmond asked nastily.

'Dreadfully,' she said. When first we practise to deceive, she thought, oh, what a something web we weave.

She was tired and confused, as only an inept liar can be; she was exhausted by questions.

'And are you settled down there – in your prison? Mother asked me most particularly to report that. I shall be obliged to write something.'

In this case, blood was thinner than water, Mrs Palfrey thought, knowing that Ludo would not have spoken to her in such an offensive, offhand way.

'I can just as well tell your mother direct,' she said. 'We *are* in communication.'

She could find no patience for this pompous grandson; her love lay elsewhere. She had quite liked him as a little boy, she remembered. Or had she made the most of what she had? She gave him a sideways glance. He was getting thin on top already, she noticed – for grass does not grow on a busy thoroughfare.

A large drop of rain fell on the pavement before them, then some more. He took off his spectacles and wiped them on a large silk handkerchief, and hurried, as if she could alter her pace to match his. Ludo would not have behaved like that. She remembered *him* holding her elbow, and keeping the umbrella carefully over her, matching his step to hers. The night of the supper-party. That wonderful evening. There had been no others.

I shan't sleep tonight, she thought, as thunder broke out.

They were getting wet and Desmond did not like it. Mrs Palfrey thought that she had been through so much in the last three-quarters of an hour that rain, even on her navy crêpe, did not matter. She enjoyed his discomfort, so much more than she could deplore her own.

'Well, the last thing I thought I should be doing this evening was walking about in South Kensington in a thunderstorm with my Granny,' he said, resigning himself to keeping pace with her. He might instead have finished his chapter on embroidery, he thought.

'It seems an awfully noisy place,' he said, as they came back to the traffic. 'I should have thought somewhere quiet and peaceful in Bournemouth or Torquay, or somewhere like that, would have been better for you.' Not that he cared.

'Peace and quiet are the last things old people want,' said Mrs Palfrey. 'We like to be where something's going on.'

'And what about those old ones in the lounge we weren't allowed to disturb on any account?'

Oh, he *is* a rude young man, she thought: refused to answer him: could not. He would quite have shamed her at the Claremont. She was so relieved to have had Ludo there instead of him.

'I expect you'll be able to get a taxi,' she said, at the foot of the steps.

'As I'm already wet through, I certainly shan't waste the money. I shall go by Underground from Gloucester Road.'

'Splendid,' she said, 'and thank you for coming.' She made her way up the steps.

'Thank you for the walk,' he called after her.

'Mrs Palfrey, you're soaked!' cried Mrs de Salis, who was in the vestibule, giving an order for her breakfast in bed. 'We wondered what on *earth* had become of you.'

'I hardly expected such a downpour.'

'It was forecast,' Mr Osmond said, standing by the door and looking down at the lights blurred on the wet road. '"Skettered rine," *she* said. That accent! I can't think why they have her.' He wondered if he should write to the *Daily Telegraph* about her, although he had had practically no luck with the *Daily Telegraph*. Many, many years ago, long before he had come to the Claremont, it had printed a letter of his about the distribution of *Fritillaria Meleagris* in the South of England, and of the interesting derivation of its name – a scholarly letter he had been proud of. Since then letters on decimalisation, fluoridation, artificial insemination, the migration of birds, racial integration, drugs and thuggery (with the interesting derivation of the word 'thug') had all been ignored.

Mrs Palfrey collected her key from the desk and passed her handkerchief over her damp face. Someone, up above, had left the lift door open, and Summers went pounding upstairs in a temper to close it.

Mrs Burton, on her blundering way to bed, joined Mr Osmond at the door. 'My, it's really tipping down,' she said.

As you've been doing all the evening, he thought, edging

away from her in dislike. She was getting worse, he decided. Mrs de Salis was having a bad effect by keeping them up much later, so that more was drunk by Mrs Burton as they all chatted, chatted. What happens to all the old men? he wondered, as he often did. He supposed that they were dead. The fact that he lingered on among the ladies made him feel epicene, isolated.

'You kept your gorgeous grandson from us,' Mrs de Salis said. Having ordered her orange juice and scrambled eggs, she joined Mrs Palfrey at the lift gate. Her voice sank very low upon the word 'gorgeous'.

Thinks she's sexy, I wouldn't be surprised, thought Mr Osmond.

'Only this once,' Mrs Palfrey said. 'We had some family business to discuss.' She shivered.

'You need a hot bath,' Mrs de Salis said. 'And order a hot whisky and lemon to be sent up.'

'Oh, no!' Mrs Palfrey said. 'I'll have the bath, though, if the water's still all right.' She never ordered anything to be sent to her room. There was an extra charge for it.

The lift came whining down and Summers, cursing, clashed back both the gates.

Desmond did not, that evening, finish his chapter on Cycladic embroidery. Having hung his wet clothes to dry, put on his dressing-gown, he switched on a lamp under a black shade in his dark, dark room and wrote to his mother, knowing that he would never sleep with so much indignation in his head. Better, he thought, to get it down on paper.

'No more wild-goose chases, please!' he began. (It was very

beautiful italic handwriting.) He went on to declare that his grandmother was dotty. 'Barred the way; bundled me down the steps. Almost as if she were ashamed of me, or of where she *was*; although from what I was allowed to see it appeared very clean and respectable, more than somewhat, really. An admirable sort of hotel for an elderly lady. However, she says I am not to go again, so don't blame me if I don't. I can't cope with your long-range charity. All the same, I am a little mystified, a little taken up with what goes on there. Odd behaviour always fascinates me, and this behaviour – *her* behaviour – was odd in the extreme. I might just, some time, if I am in that ghastly part of London, pop in (*your* phrase) again. And take a raincoat next time. I am sneezing already. Incidentally, apart from everything else, Grannie has become a very, very rude old lady.'

He had a sense of unreality, as if he were doing something completely out of character, by writing to a mother in Scotland, about a grandmother in the Cromwell Road – two places which seemed quite irrelevant to him. He had always had a leaning to an Anglo-Irish background (almost felt it his due), or, even, Anglo-French. (Guinnesses or Hennessys would do.) He wanted to suggest casual grandeur derived from true grandeur, and he longed to be in the line of intellectual forebears (instead of half sport, half slogger) – to be not the only one in the family who ever mentioned Proust or Joyce. What he could achieve from hard work he already had. Grandmothers he had envisaged, ancient, high-born, eccentric (not quite the same as dotty), laying down the law or placing their bets. What he particularly did *not* want was an old party, poor on her feet, keeping him company on a rainy,

London walk – and resenting it, too, he was obliged to admit to himself.

Mrs Burton felt as if she were swimming along the corridor towards her bedroom, glancing off the walls like a balloon, gliding past pairs of shoes put out to be cleaned. She pulled up at number fifty-three, steadied herself, made a forwards movement with the key. Calmly does it. Miraculously, she hit the keyhole first time. She opened the door and entered the room with dignity. Once in, she sat down in the armchair and stared in front of her, listening to something she could not place ticking with regularity in her head. What could it be? Her watch? She raised her wrist to her screwed-up eyes and thought that it might be eleven o'clock, or five to twelve. A pleasant evening it had been. And conversation. She liked conversation, but could not remember what it had been about.

Presently, she shivered. Her hands were cold and shaky, and she would have liked a hot water bottle, but it was beyond her to organise such a thing. Instead, she got up and took a flask of brandy from her top drawer. She poured some into a tooth glass and drank it quickly as if it were medicine, still holding the flask in her other hand, at the ready.

After the second drink, she sat on the side of the bed and kicked off a shoe.

She began to sing in a wavering voice:

'I love the moon. I love the sun.
I love the forest – the flowers – the fun.'

She broke off and glared at the wardrobe which seemed to be advancing on her, closing in.

'The forest, the flowers, the fun,' she repeated, suddenly puzzled by the meaningless string of words.

Then she sagged, slumped. With a last effort she snatched at her other shoe, threw it across the room and, saying 'Bugger it', fell back upon the bed and closed her eyes.

13

Mr Osmond was now beset on all sides – or so it seemed to him – by busy chatter. Mrs de Salis was the instigator of it – the talk about hats and hairdressers, the summer sales, fashions at Ascot, and Royalty, Royalty, Royalty. There was always something in the newspapers to set that talk going. The Queen Mother topped – here at the Claremont – the popularity poll. Her air of independence was taken as an inspiration to them all. 'Though money helps. There's no gainsaying it,' said Mrs Post, and sighed. It seemed to her that only straitened means prevented her from having just such a colourful widowhood – salmon-fishing in waders, film premières, in tiara and lace crinoline; or talking in paddocks to horses and trainers and jockeys. It was a life as remote from the Claremont as almost anything could be; but was vicariously lived there, and admired.

Rubbish, thought Mr Osmond. Poppycock and twaddle. And to take part in such balderdash only Mrs Palfrey, he observed, seemed disinclined.

'I don't envy them their job,' was all she had to say upon the Royal matter.

'But of course not!' The other ladies came dashing in; for it went without saying that none of them – nor the meanest and most miserable of its subjects – would ever envy the Royal family its job.

On a summer's evening, they sat about in the lounge discussing the Queen. There had been one of the usual Ascot thunderstorms and in the evening newspapers there was a photograph of Her Majesty making her way to the paddock under a large black umbrella. Everything looked grey and awash; pale shoes were ruined, floppy hats had flopped.

Mrs Burton had won something in the region of seventy-five shillings on the big race. Summers had carried the bet for her. Mrs de Salis had backed (with her own bookie, she rather grandly explained) a horse called Maisonette; but she searched the stop press vainly for its name. 'Perhaps it didn't run,' she said, not in a hopeful voice.

Mrs Post had never put money on a horse in her life, and the very idea of doing so alarmed her. Mrs Palfrey would not have dreamed of betting off the course.

'Her face looks so set, even grim,' said Mrs de Salis, re-examining the photograph of the Queen. 'Of course, *he* doesn't like it; only goes on sufferance, I have heard. Dear little hat!' She turned a page, and read out, 'Turquoise.'

Mr Osmond, sipping his before-dinner wine, sat back and watched them.

'They're partial to turquoise,' Mrs Burton said.

'Oh, it's England at its best,' Mrs de Salis suddenly burst out, laying aside the picture of pouring rain. 'Gold Cup Day.

The salmon and strawberries. The band playing. Champagne.'

'Oh, *wouldn't* it rain!' Mrs Post said, looking at the streaming window. She was thinking of herself now, and not of the Royal family at Ascot. She was waiting for a cousin to arrive. A summer's evening drive had been promised, with a picnic. It was a yearly occurrence, and gave the cousin who was ten years younger than Mrs Post, a sense of duty done which might last her, with any luck, for the following twelve months.

Mrs de Salis leaned forward and put a hand on Mrs Post's wrist, as if to both steady her and rally her. 'Now don't fuss,' she said. 'You're going to have a lovely evening.'

For Mrs Post could not help looking, first at her watch, and then at the weather. The rain seemed quite relentless. They would have to sit in the car, perhaps in Richmond Park, to eat their fish-paste sandwiches. It was not going to be what she had looked forward to.

When Antonio brought Mrs Burton's third whisky-and-soda, Mrs Post, on an impulse, asked him for a glass of sherry, to pass the waiting-time and cheer her up for her dismal excursion. Cousin was decidedly late.

'Is your visitor late, dear?' Mrs de Salis asked.

'Oh, a minute or so; but my watch may be fast.'

They all compared their watches, and referred themselves to Mr Osmond's, which gave the date as well and was much marvelled at and called upon.

'Please God, let her come soon,' Mrs Post was praying. As the minutes ticked by, she suffered Mrs de Salis's probing glances. Suddenly – was it the sherry? – she said: 'As one gets older life becomes all take and no give. One relies on other people for the treats and things. It's like being an infant again.'

Mrs de Salis looked at her in consternation, and Mrs Palfrey with concern. This was not Claremont talk.

'But *you've* done the giving *earlier*," Mrs de Salis pointed out.

'Not always to the same people,' Mrs Post insisted.

'It all works out, you know,' said Mrs de Salis. 'In the scheme of things,' she added vaguely. 'Bread upon the water.'

'Being *taken out*, I mean, as if one were a school-child.' Mrs Post put her fist to her mouth. She thought bitterly of sitting there, waiting for someone to turn up, out of the kindness of their heart. Will they come? Or won't they, and so make one-self a fool? '*I* don't take people out any more,' she said aloud. All wished that she would stop. 'I wouldn't know where to take them. Of course, it's nice to be given a treat, but not if it's *always* that way round.'

Mrs de Salis looked at the half-full sherry glass, as if esti-mating how much it was to be blamed for this turn in the conversation.

'Oh, come off it!' Mrs Burton said robustly. 'You *are* in the dumps. It's this bloody weather.'

Mr Osmond saw Mrs Palfrey glance down and aside, and he approved of her doing so.

'Anyway, for my part it just isn't true,' Mrs Burton went on. 'I and my brother-in-law always stand treat in turn.'

'We haven't *all*,' said Mr Osmond heavily, 'got a brother-in-law who would tolerate such a situation.'

Mrs Palfrey had lost the thread of the conversation and began to turn the rings on her fingers, examining them with great interest, as if she had never seen them before.

Mrs Burton, for a while, appeared to be offended about her brother-in-law, but was only pretending. Taking umbrage was something not in her nature. 'Now, don't be so old-fashioned,' was all she said to Mr Osmond, who set his lips together and looked steadily at Mrs Palfrey, with whom he had for some time felt himself aligned. But Mrs Palfrey was not thinking of him. She, too, was praying for Mrs Post's cousin to arrive. It was nearly dinner-time.

The rain had stopped.

The receptionist put her head into the room and announced that Mrs Post was wanted on the telephone.

'Oh, it is my cousin, I expect,' Mrs Post said, hurrying from the room, her head ducked down.

'Dear me!' Mrs de Salis said, after a silence. 'I hope she's not going to be disappointed, let down. She seems in such unusually low spirits that a change of scenery is the only thing to buck her up.'

'Well, *I* shall go in to dinner,' Mrs Palfrey said firmly, making a move, and lessening, by one at least, the group which Mrs Post would have to face on her return. Mr Osmond opened the door for her, and followed: but Mrs de Salis and Mrs Burton decided to sit on a little longer.

When Mrs Post quite soon returned, she looked jaunty.

'Well, that's rather a relief,' she said. 'Brenda thinks it isn't a very nice evening for a drive out. It will be better to wait for settled weather.'

'Yes, of course,' said Mrs Burton.

But now the sun had come out and Mrs de Salis turned her head to the window to look at it.

*

During dinner, Mr Osmond had an idea, so sudden, so perfect, that he sat with his napkin to his lips for several seconds, staring down at his empty plate, pondering the possibility.

Then excitement began to work in him. His stomach seemed to be churning up the mushroom omelette. (He ate sparingly.) Acid gurglings he could not stop. A dish of ice-cream was placed before him, and he began to take sips of it, off the little spoon. He did not glance at Mrs Palfrey's table, but he was blushing all the same. He felt – not fear; it was alarm, really. Later, he realised that he had eaten strawberry ice-cream, although he had ordered vanilla. Usually, he would have made quite an issue of it, but this evening had not identified the flavour until it was too late.

Coffee very few of these old regulars drank. It kept them awake they said; and it cost extra.

One by one, they stirred, they slowly rose, they made off towards knitting or crossword puzzles (in one case, brandy), and, such had things come to, probably more talk about Queen Elizabeth, the Queen Mother.

How to get Mrs Palfrey alone, out of earshot, Mr Osmond wondered. Having had his inspiration, he felt that he would never sleep without knowing the outcome.

By some miracle, she was the last to get up.

The middle-aged celebrating group had not yet come in, and Antonio and the elderly waitresses were becoming grimly restless.

Mr Osmond glanced in Mrs Palfrey's direction. She had such an air of being a gentlewoman, he decided. She ate her ginger pudding casually, as if she were unconcerned with what it was.

Now the timing had to be exact, he realised. He must reach

her table as she was about to get up from it. Fusses like this upset his heart, and his hands began to tremble. Mrs Palfrey moved. He half rose. She searched round for, and found, a little beaded purse. She settled back, opened it, and peered into it, shut it, moved again. He, having leaned back, waiting, suddenly shifted, and slightly pulled a muscle in his calf. She was now definitely getting up. He followed, limping. She was almost regal, he thought, trying to intercept her.

As she was about to pass through the door, having said 'Thank you' in a gracious voice to her waitress, he was able to step forward before Antonio and hold it open for her.

'Ah, Mr Osmond, thank you. Now we must go and take sides about Princess Margaret again, I suppose,' she said.

For that I love you, he thought. During his time at the Claremont there had been no *rapport* with anyone – attempts at it with waiters, porters, even the manager, but all one-sided, the attempts forced on others, and rejected. Women he usually tried to avoid, but Mrs Palfrey looked so wonderfully like a man, and had an air of behaving like one. Trivia (one of his favourite words) she appeared to scorn.

'I realise you have been suffering, too,' he said, walking very slowly towards the lounge. 'It isn't the same since Mrs What's-her-name arrived. No more of those peaceful evenings.'

'Some people obviously think it is better,' she said, matching her pace to his.

'I never cease to marvel how things get so much worse as one grows older. Everything! Everywhere one turns. Even a little quiet is now denied one.'

'Oh, come!' she said, smiling encouragingly, turning stiffly to look at him. What he called a reliable face.

They were nearing the lounge, and he would now have to blurt out what he would have preferred to lead up to.

'Mrs Palfrey,' he heard himself saying, rather loudly although, apart from Mrs de Salis, she had the best hearing at the Claremont. 'Would you do me the honour of being my guest at a Masonic do?'

Mrs Palfrey looked a little startled. 'I thought those were for men only, and highly secret,' she said.

'It is a Ladies' Night. I have no partner, so I rarely go. But should like to.'

It was all of sixty years since any man had asked her to go out with him. (Arthur had never issued invitations; he had let her know what was expected.) She wished that *this* invitation could have come in writing, to give her more time to decide.

'It is not for some weeks,' Mr Osmond said, watching her. 'I simply wanted to make my plans and look forward to them.'

Mrs Palfrey, like most women, could not help her thoughts turning to what she could wear on such an occasion. She thought of her fur cape. That, and the invitation itself, and the stir it would cause if she accepted it, persuaded her at last to smile and nod.

'Why, it would make a very nice change and a new experience for me,' she said.

'My wife always enjoyed the evenings.'

'And I am sure that I shall, too.'

As their conversation was over, Mrs Palfrey walked on past the door of the lounge and stood looking out at the Cromwell Road. It was a beautiful evening now, and sun streamed in through the dusty glass of the revolving doors.

Mr Osmond hesitated, then went to take his usual chair apart from where the ladies sat. When Mrs Palfrey entered the room later, they did not glance at one another.

She sat down beside Mrs Post, who was subdued. To take her mind off the exasperating change in the weather, Mrs Palfrey began a conversation about literature. As Mrs Arbuthnot's library-runner, Mrs Post had always been deferred to in this matter. She had built up a reputation as an authority from her little chats with library assistants and knew, as she put it, what *went*.

'My grandson, who works at the British Museum, as you know, is ambitious to write a novel,' Mrs Palfrey said. 'In fact he is, I believe, quite far gone in one.'

'Oh, I shall look forward to seeing that on the shelf,' Mrs Post exclaimed. She could talk of knowing the author to the librarian.

'I shall hope for it to be taken *off* the shelf from time to time,' Mrs Palfrey said, in a soft, amused voice.

'The things that *go*, you know! It's no criterion. So often not at all what you and I would want to read – or your grandson would want to write!' She sighed, and for some reason glanced across at Mr Osmond. 'The baser element, you know. There's such a great deal of the baser element these days. Miss Taylor at the library agrees with me. I shall never forget how, in my ignorance, I brought back one of those to Mrs Arbuthnot. It was called *All Done By Mirrors*, and so, of course, I thought it must be a detective. A sort of Agatha Christie title, don't you agree? But it was not, and I was never allowed to forget it, as you can probably imagine.'

Mrs Palfrey nodded.

'"They shouldn't allow such scum to be published", Mrs Arbuthnot kept saying.'

'As she had her eyes glued to the page, perhaps,' Mrs Palfrey suggested.

'Well, she finished it, and then handed it back to me as if she hardly liked touching it. Is your grandson historical? I do hope he is historical.'

Before Mrs Palfrey could find any sort of answer to this, Ludo himself appeared at the open door and looked about him. Mrs Palfrey made a sweeping, traffic-policeman's gesture, and he came across the lounge and bent and kissed her soft and wrinkled cheek. It was so long since she had seen him that she felt put out, in a panic almost. She had been trying hard lately to forget him, like a young girl with an unresponsive, but beloved, boy. This evening was turning out to be a tiring and exciting one.

'Mrs Post and I were just talking of you,' she said, and then, trying to right herself, added, 'in a general way that we were talking about books.'

'Are you historical?' Mrs Post asked eagerly. She had by now quite put aside her regrets about the evening out in Richmond Park.

Ludo, whose eyes, Mrs Palfrey noticed, seemed not to be seeing anything, said in a tired voice, 'I'm not sure that I know much about history.'

Mrs Post, for the first time that evening – and for a long time – exulted. She knew perfectly well that in her kindness, Mrs Palfrey had condescended to her, and thought now that she would do a little condescending herself.

'I should have thought,' she began, 'though I'm not scholarly, of course ... you must forgive me; but the British Museum must be the place above all to get to grips with it.'

Ludo, fidgeting so nervously that Mrs Palfrey got up and pressed the bell for Antonio, said, 'I suppose I'm only interested in Mary Queen of Scots and Bonnie Prince Charlie. And they've been done.' Then, looking up quite dazedly at Antonio said, to Mrs Palfrey's consternation, 'Oh, anything. Bring me anything you like.'

'Yes, of course,' said Mrs Post, 'and what a shame for you. They have been done indeed.'

'A glass of brandy,' Mrs Palfrey said, looking steadily at Antonio.

'And *now*,' cried Mrs de Salis, coming forward, 'we can at last see your gorgeous grandson.' To Ludo, who had got up tiredly, she said, 'The last time you slipped through our fingers and went out walking.'

Ludo wondered what she was talking about. He smiled vaguely, hoping to stave her off, but she settled herself in a near-by chair.

'I rather wanted to be speaking to you privately,' he said presently in a low voice to Mrs Palfrey. 'And so you did last time,' Mrs de Salis said, for, after all, she had the best hearing at the Claremont. 'And you got your poor grandmother soaking wet into the bargain. She might have caught pneumonia but for my advice to have hot whisky sent up to her in bed.'

Mrs Palfrey was in a horrid panic and Ludo looked dazed.

Mr Osmond, wondering if he, too, might go over and have a word with them, had decided not to. As far as Mrs Palfrey was concerned, he would rest on his laurels.

'She's so right, your grandmother,' said Mrs de Salis. 'To

dote on you, I mean.' To Ludo's consternation, she suddenly put out a hand and stroked the back of his head teasingly.

Mr Osmond looked at her with loathing, irritation and jealousy; and Mrs Palfrey did the same.

Ludo took his brandy from Antonio's tray and began to sip it, glad of something to do.

'And now I've embarrassed him,' Mrs de Salis said, adding to her impropriety, as embarrassing people do. 'It's an old woman's privilege, you know.' She laughed as if the thought of herself as an old woman amused her, and must amuse everybody else.

'To embarrass people, you mean?' Mr Osmond asked loudly, from his distance.

Mrs de Salis let her eyes rest on him for a moment or two, and there was a shade of menace in her look.

'If I had gone on my picnic, I should have missed you,' Mrs Post said happily to Ludo. 'As we did before, of course. And we see so few young people.'

'*This* one has been kept purposely from us,' Mrs de Salis said.

'I think ... when you have finished your brandy, my dear, we might go for a little stroll,' Mrs Palfrey suggested, and at once Ludo drained his glass and stood up. He helped Mrs Palfrey to her feet.

'Oh, what indefatigable walkers you both are,' said Mrs de Salis, sounding cross. 'I feel you are being hustled away from us,' she told Ludo. 'You are always being hustled away from us.'

Mrs Palfrey was walking towards the door. She could not get out of the room quickly enough.

*

'It was Desmond,' Mrs Palfrey explained, as they walked towards the gardens. 'He simply arrived one evening, and I had to smuggle him out quickly before anyone could see him. It upset me.'

'How dangerously you live. And he might come again,' Ludo said.

'No, I told him not to.'

'How on earth did you do that?'

'I said that it was inconvenient. That there is nowhere to receive visitors. After all, there isn't. What a beautiful evening!'

Ludo did not seem to notice the softness of the light, the gilded windows, the roses drying out in the gardens of the square. He was nervy, as a bee is in bad weather. And Mrs Palfrey began to feel edgy herself.

'There has been a calamity,' he said. 'I came to tell you about it.'

Before she could think of the calamity itself, she felt a little pride in his wish to confide. It lasted no time.

'Is it to do with – with – Rosie?' she asked, with distaste but resolution in her voice. She had almost said 'that Rosie'. Getting into trouble was the sort of trouble one associated with the young these days.

Ludo, seemingly mystified, said, 'Rosie? No, not Rosie. Why Rosie?'

'I simply wondered,' Mrs Palfrey said primly.

Ludo considered this for a moment – shook his head. 'No, I'm afraid the Major has skedaddled.'

'What Major?'

'From the love-nest. My mother's, you know. I surely told you.'

Ah, so his mother was the calamity. Hers was the trouble. Mrs Palfrey felt enormous relief. But she was tired. Side-stepping from a dog's mess, she stumbled a little. He took her arm.

'Oh, if only one had a key and could get into the gardens and sit on one of those seats. I feel like Alice in Wonderland about it.'

'That's Blighty for you.'

'I think I must go home . . . back . . . now,' Mrs Palfrey said. 'It has been what I believe young people call quite a day.' No doubt her daughter up in Scotland imagined her rotting away hour by hour, doing nothing, nothing happening. 'I am sorry about your mother. Is she much put out?'

'"Put out", to be taken literally.'

They turned at the corner of the Square to make the return journey.

'Why did this Major leave her? Although it is certainly no business of mine.'

'I'm afraid he's in some sort of bother about money with his business-partner. As soon as there's that sort of bother, everything else emerges. I doubt if my mother will ever see him again, though I don't tell *her* that.'

'The Major sounds a bit of a bounder,' Mrs Palfrey said, coming up with one of her husband's words.

'Keeping two homes going,' Ludo said vaguely. 'Not having paid the Putney rent for some time, it appears. He might go to prison for this business.'

'Oh, dear.' Mrs Palfrey sighed, but really for herself and not the Major. The sun had gone now, and it was the end of a long day.

'It was nice of you to come to confide in me,' she said, plodding on.

At this, Ludo looked more downcast than ever.

'Well, she certainly can't come to me,' he said briskly, but as if he were arguing with himself. 'She will have to go to my aunt's in Wimbledon. She can stay there for a week or two, until they have one of their quarrels.'

To Mrs Palfrey she sounded a tiresome and feckless woman.

'There are all her things in Putney,' Ludo said. 'How to get all that junk away while she still owes the rent? She can hardly steal away in the middle of the night with it, and the landlord sleeping in the flat below.'

'I should think not,' said Mrs Palfrey, and then wondered if this tone of righteousness became her. She had herself practised to deceive.

'Parents should lead their own lives,' Ludo grumbled.

Mrs Palfrey, who was doing so, was silent.

'She has nothing put by?' she presently suggested. It was all beginning to appear more of her business than she could have believed.

'Well, she never *had* much. The Major was mean, except with drink. Plenty of that. She had this silly little part-time job. Well, that won't do any more, of course.'

'My means are rather limited,' Mrs Palfrey began, and Ludo looked at her with a sort of glum hope, 'but for your sake alone ... although it is hardly my concern, as I have said ...'

And then – to her, a miracle; to him it seemed disaster – a taxi came slowly down the road towards them, and Mrs Palfrey put her last strength into a large beckoning wave of her arm.

'I'm sorry, but my day has proved too much for me,' she apologised. 'The Claremont Hotel,' she said to the driver, who looked surprised, for it was hardly two hundred yards away. In fact, he had just dropped two Americans there.

Ludo helped Mrs Palfrey into the cab; but, before he could shut the door, she leaned forward and said, 'Fifty pounds.'

He felt a sudden fury with his mother, and he blushed.

'In the post tomorrow,' Mrs Palfrey said, and slammed the door. She had meant to say 'as a loan'. Now it was too late.

Ludo's mother had humiliated them both, had threatened their relationship. He, striding away along the street, frowning, thought, When my book is published, I'll pay it back, and with interest. Then he remembered that his book would displease Mrs Palfrey more than any debts. He had banked on her being dead – or out of his life – before it saw the light of day.

Mrs Palfrey leaned back for a moment and closed her eyes. From capital, she thought. She was beginning to do the thing she knew that she must never do: for some unknown woman of loose morals and, worse than that, untidy thinking.

Once, Arthur had talked about arranging annuities, but had died too soon to do so. It was men's business. Money was to do with *them*. Woman had not the chance to practise until it was too late. She wondered, as the cab drew up, so quickly, before the Claremont, if Mr Osmond knew about such things. London bank managers she imagined as far too alarming to consult. They would explain; but she would not grasp.

In the Claremont vestibule two Americans stood looking lost, bewildered, beside a heap of their admirably matching luggage.

Mrs Burton and Mrs de Salis still sat in the lounge.

Mrs Palfrey took her key, and made her way to the lift.

'Will we have a drink before we go up?' the American husband asked his wife, looking round doubtfully, as if uncertain if he could arrange it.

Fawn-coloured, the woman's face; exhausted from travelling. 'Why now, Pete,' she said dully, 'I don't believe I will.'

14

Well, that's the last we shall ever see of *her*,' Mr Osmond said, having curtly waved goodbye to Mrs de Salis from the steps of the Claremont. Mrs Post had gone on waving wistfully until the taxi could no longer be distinguished from others in the traffic-jam.

'Oh, I shall miss her,' she cried, at last. 'She made us all feel young.'

'For myself, I shall not grieve,' Mr Osmond said in a low voice to Mrs Palfrey in the hall. She had been the first to go inside, rather like the Queen turning away from the Palace balcony after the fly-past.

But it was *not* the last they were to see of Mrs de Salis. Like quite a few show-off people, she sometimes kept her word, and surprised everybody by doing so. The effect was that of a well-proved liar's saying something later found to be true – sending all the premises topsy-turvy. Mrs de Salis had always been disturbing.

'What is plonk?' Mrs Post asked nervously one morning.

After breakfast, they all had invitation cards in their hands, on which champagne glasses were dizzily scattered, with haphazard bubbles rising from them, drink salutations in various European languages were printed slant-wise between, and the whole suggestion of sophistication was puzzling to all save Mrs Burton.

However, it was Mr Osmond who answered Mrs Post. 'Plonk,' he said, 'is something dire. Never to be drunk.'

'It says "Plonk for all who come",' Mrs Post read, her nervousness increased.

'She must be joking,' Mrs Burton hoped aloud.

During the next few days, Mrs de Salis's party was scarcely mentioned. Acceptances were sent off on the sly.

'Are you *going*?' Mrs Post at last dared to ask Mr Osmond, who had said at the start that he would not. (*Where* was taken for granted.)

'I suppose one must be civil. I dare say I shall look in.'

'I was wondering if it might not be possible for us all to share a taxi. Inverness Crescent is quite a little ride from here. I was asking Summers about it.'

In spite of all her talk, Mrs de Salis had ended up on what Mr Osmond had lost no time in calling 'the wrong side of the Park'.

It was not until tea-time on the very day of the party that the question of the taxi was mentioned again, and it was to Mrs Post's great relief that it was.

'I suppose it would be rather foolish for us not to go together,' Mr Osmond said.

'It would be plain bloody daft,' said Mrs Burton.

Mr Osmond put the tips of his fingers together and looked at Mrs Palfrey, waiting for her opinion, and ignoring Mrs Burton.

'I agree with you,' Mrs Palfrey said.

'Then let us meet in the hall at – say – ten to six – and Summers can whistle up a cab.'

No one consulted Mrs Post, who kept nodding excitedly.

'It will take more than ten minutes to get across to Bayswater,' Mrs Burton pointed out.

'We are bidden for six o'clock. I think for nice timing we should aim at ten past,' said Mr Osmond. Not to seem too eager, he thought.

'Oh, I hope he'll be able to get a cab,' Mrs Post began, with fresh anguish. 'Just about six o'clock – the worst possible time.' She could hardly contain this new anxiety.

'Ten to six, then,' Mr Osmond said masterfully. He got up and went to the door. I will sit on one of the little tip-up seats, he thought. Opposite Mrs Palfrey. I will hand *her* in first.

He went up to his room to put on his best, dark, pin-striped suit, his old school tie.

Mrs Post also hastened away. There was only an hour in which to get changed, although everything was laid out in her bedroom, and she had already attended to her nails – buffed them strenuously and pushed back cuticles, with instruments from her girlhood's manicure-set, which must surely confuse any future archaeologists of the South Kensington dig.

Mrs Palfrey left later, with a more leisurely tread.

Mrs Burton remained, reading a magazine. She, for one, was going as she was, since she was always dressed as if in readiness for a cocktail party, with plenty of dark, draped dresses and costume jewellery. She came down to breakfast thus.

Mrs Post furtively tilted a bottle of lavender-water on to a corner of her handkerchief.

Mrs Palfrey winced, sliding a foot into one of her best glacé kid shoes.

Mr Osmond straightened his tie and leaned forwards and grinned at himself in the mirror, seemed fairly satisfied.

Mrs Burton had rung the bell for a quick one.

Summers was more than five minutes trying to get a taxi, and Mrs Post began to wring her hands and fear that they would never get away. She read the menu over and over again, but seemed unable to take it in. It might be in a foreign language, she thought – which, indeed, it approximately was. And dinner itself seemed unreal to her, when so much was to happen first.

They caused quite a little stir, the four of them, and Mr Wilkins, the manager, came to see them off. Mrs Burton overheard a passing guest saying to another, 'Aren't they *sweet?*' and nearly burst with rage.

At last, they were down the steps and into the cab and, as they drove off, Mrs Post sat watching the meter and clutching her purse, so that she should be ready with her share of the fare – and the tip, oh, what about the tip – as soon as they arrived.

Mrs Palfrey had calmly decided to settle up with Mr Osmond later, and when they were alone. This seemed to her discreet. In this new world where women must be expected to pay for things, one had to make up rules for oneself which, in one's youth, had been decided differently. Having to do this unaccustomed thing, she relied for guidance on common sense and consideration, as she always had.

She guessed that Mrs Burton would make a fuss, waving about a pound note and wondering if anyone had change.

But Mr Osmond's way of dropping his hand in a chopping-off gesture forbade any discussion as, having paid the fare, he stood aside to follow them across the pavement. Mrs Post was glad of her nylon fur coat. There was quite a little nip in the air, as she had hoped there would be.

The houses in Inverness Crescent had recently been painted. Pillared and porticoed now in dazzling white, and with window-boxes of public-gardens' flowers of orange and beetroot red, they looked conscious of their rescue from threatened desuetude and decay, looked, for the time-being, most imposing.

Mr Osmond rang the bell under the name De Salis, and held his better ear close to the little grille.

'*Entrez!*' remotely trilled Mrs de Salis's voice.

I wouldn't have known what to do, Mrs Post thought, and looked thankfully at Mr Osmond.

He put a hand to the front door and it swung magically inwards.

The hall had black and white tiles and an arrangement of plastic flowers on a table. Music came from an opened door on the first floor, to which they rather breathlessly climbed. And there was Mrs de Salis waiting with arms outspread to welcome them.

'Oh, it is like old times,' she cried.

Each one, as they approached, she kissed or, rather, laid her cheek to theirs. Mr Osmond, coming last, held out his hand. 'You shan't escape,' she said, and gave his pink cheek, in passing, a little smear of lipstick.

Well, that's starting off on the wrong foot with a vengeance, he thought.

The ladies were taken into Mrs de Salis's bedroom to leave their coats. Mrs Post's eyes darted about, noting pink-frilled valance, buttoned satin, enormous scent-spray ... no, there was no time to notice any more. Mrs Palfrey patted her hair with her large hands, and seemed ready for the fray. Mrs Burton lifted her skirt and tugged at her roll-on. 'Well, girls,' she said, 'let's get at it.'

'Red or white?' they were asked by Mrs de Salis's adorable Willie, who could not have been recognised from the photograph they had been shown at the Claremont. His hair had receded, his once-pretty, sensuous face was now pouchy, with dark shadows under the eyes.

The bottles, as Mr Osmond had already noted, were turned so that the labels were away from gaze, and when Willie lifted one to pour out, he swathed it in a napkin, as if it were champagne. A nice touch, Mr Osmond thought grimly.

Willie was drinking some amber-coloured drink in a large glass which he often topped up in what Mr Osmond supposed was the kitchen. From there, he brought out a dish of peanuts.

There were two other guests, a large and jolly woman, whom Willie addressed as Aunt Bunty, and an elderly actress, of whom Mrs Post alone had heard. She was there to impress the guests from the Claremont and clearly understood this role, and at once began to dazzle and fascinate.

Mr Osmond stood near to Willie, wondering once more, what could have happened to all the old men. An ancient filthy story came to mind, and he was about to share it with his only ally, when he saw Mrs Palfrey standing by the window, and he felt ashamed. He told Willie instead a very slightly risqué one he had heard on the wireless. Willie laughed excessively. 'Oh, I can see, sir, you're one of us,' he said. He would not let up on the 'sir'. When one's old, Mr Osmond suddenly marvelled, no one calls you by your Christian name. You might just as well not have it.

Mrs Palfrey – who, for a moment or two, had paused by the large window, looking at plane trees – felt unsettled. After hotel life, this flat seemed so personal, in spite of the anonymity of its furnishings; so free and yet a haven. She felt a transitory longing for such a home, where she might potter from room to room and take her own time over everything, even entertain a little – Ludo to dinner; her Claremont friends for sherry. Yet she knew that she was past all hope of it. She began to feel tired as she reviewed the idea: she thought of the stairs, and the shopping, and the cleaning and washing-up, taps needing washers, pipes freezing, window-cleaners not arriving, no one arriving.

She had never been a good cook, for in the East it had been done for her. To say the Rottingdean meals had lacked variety was the kindest way her efforts could have been described. She knew it and did not want to have to try again.

The music came softly through – 'Some Enchanted Evening'. Mrs Burton had gone from humming, to singing the words, would soon dance a few steps, Mr Osmond thought.

'Now, Bunty!' Mrs de Salis said at Mrs Palfrey's elbow. And

there was Bunty dragged up from her chair and brought over to mingle a bit and be introduced. 'Here is Mrs Palfrey. And this is my sister-in-law, Bunty, who lives in an hotel in Brighton.'

'Adore Brighton,' Bunty said.

'She's come to stay for three days only, and that will be that, and nothing will persuade her to stop a minute longer.'

'She wears me out,' Bunty explained to Mrs Palfrey. (Mrs de Salis pouted, but looked not unpleased.) 'We always end up squabbling.'

Yes, Mrs Palfrey could understand this. She gave a smile which meant nothing, and took a cautious sip of her wine.

'Bickies?' Mrs de Salis had been to fetch some. Mrs Palfrey took one. Bunty scooped up a handful.

'Adore anything cheesy,' she said.

'You're crafty,' Mrs Burton said to Willie, looking at his glass.

'Not allowed wine, my dear lady,' he said. 'Gout.'

'My sympathies. I suffer from it myself,' Mrs Burton lied.

'Yes, it's very nasty. Not nice. Not nice at all. Will you have a peanut?'

Mrs Burton looked scornfully at the peanuts and did not answer him.

'I well remember you as Mrs Darling,' Mrs Post was saying. 'I took my little nephew to it. It doesn't seem possible. He's a married man with teenage children. He lives in Canada, of course. It must have been around nineteen-twenty-four, we went ... wasn't it?'

'*Much* later,' Fay Sylvester snapped. After this, she would have liked to drift away from Mrs Post, but that she seemed the only one who had ever heard of her. She decided to bully her instead of dazzling.

'Bloody awful play,' she said.

'Peter Pan?' cried Mrs Post in astonishment; then thought how people did seem to swear nowadays.

'I hate kids,' said Fay Sylvester, whose real name was Felicity Sheringham-Vincent. She wished she had not changed it, but it had seemed a good idea at the time. 'My ex-husband always said that a man who hates children cannot be entirely bad.'

Mrs Post looked like a teased child and glanced about her.

'Drink up,' Willie said in an automatic voice, as if he were a nurse administering medicine. 'Buckets of plonk we must get down us.'

'Us!' Mrs Burton heard, furiously.

'Can't face it at breakfast, d'you know.'

Well, he didn't want *this* little party, Mr Osmond calmly thought. And he's not really here.

The turned-down, muffled music ran out, and no one except Mrs Burton noticed and she felt only a vague lack of something.

'What was your favourite part?' Mrs Post went eagerly on. She had never met an actress before, and could tell her cousin all about it.

'Hedda Gabler,' Mrs Sylvester said, after a little pause to consider – nose deliciously wrinkled, she opined – one great role against another. The risk was justified.

'What was that in?' Mrs Post inquired.

'Now, you're pulling my leg,' was all that Fay Sylvester could say to this, not knowing that, in the middle of the night, Mrs Post might worry about her reply.

'You must . . . I insist . . . have one of these quite delicious peanuts,' she said.

'Yes, I will be tempted: though I'm sure I shall spoil my dinner.'

'From all that Megsy tells me of that ghastly hotel, you won't be missing much.'

'Oh, but it's quite . . .' Megsy! she thought.

'Have another nut.' Quite sharp, Fay's tone. A command.

Mrs Post considered the dish, and then carefully picked out one nut, as if it were different from the others. 'So nice,' she murmured, meaning the party, not the peanut.

'Well, we men are a bit thin on the ground,' Mr Osmond said affably to Willie.

'And this one's a bit thin on the top, too,' Willie said, matching the geniality. 'You must come over and meet old Fay.'

This was almost the last thing Mr Osmond wished to do; and, Fay, having heard the 'old', put on a couldn't care less look. She gave Willie a different look, which somehow – perhaps because she had been an actress – conveyed to him, 'Don't think I don't know about *you*.'

'Of course,' Mrs Palfrey was saying, 'there must be a lot going on in Brighton.' She sometimes considered Brighton. The winter milder. The air cleaner. The whole of the South Coast lay before her. I'm not bound to the Cromwell Road for the rest of my life, she thought – more unsettled than she knew by Mrs de Salis's flat.

'Somehow, you know, you don't *go* to it, though, what's going on, I mean,' Aunt Bunty said. 'I'll tell you something,' she said, with a sort of sideways, conspiratorial look, 'and don't repeat it beyond these four walls, still less within, I have never put my nose inside the Royal Pavilion.'

'I haven't been to the Victoria and Albert Museum,' Mrs Palfrey said, with a little smile.

'Well, why the hell should we?'

'So you were a stage-actress,' Mr Osmond said to Fay Sylvester.

She was not his idea of an actress – flat-chested, thin hair, croaky voice.

In spite of his question, she decided to enchant again. She would put one of her spells upon him. 'And what is wrong with being an actress?' she asked, in a challenging, flirtatious voice which annoyed him.

I'll play it tired, he thought. He apologised for a little yawn, looked at her through watery eyes, said, 'Nothing that I know of,' and walked towards Mrs Palfrey.

But Willie intercepted him. 'The john is through there, first on the left,' he said, pointing with a napkin-swathed bottle.

I suppose I'd better, Mr Osmond thought, annoyed with Willie for putting the idea into his head. He could join Mrs Palfrey later.

The lavatory was pink and silver, everything possible dotted with moss roses. The seat had a candlewick cover. Bloody nonsense, thought Mr Osmond, slamming it back just in the nick of time. He had to feel grudgingly grateful to Willie.

Little jointed stringy things the shape of tadpoles drifted across his vision. He had to keep blinking his eyes to get rid of them, but soon they drifted back. He had tried the white plonk (thin and acid), and then, hoping for something better, since it could hardly be worse, the red, which was blurred and cloudy.

The door handle went softly down and was at once released. On the other side, Mrs Post hastened away in consternation, wondering how much longer she could safely wait.

Mr Osmond flushed the w.c, and then sauntered about a bit in there, so that anyone interested would think that he was washing his hands, which he could not be bothered to do. He even turned on one of the taps with a great gush which Mrs Post, who had crept up again, listened to in anguish. In spite of all this messing about, passing time, he forgot to button up his flies.

He opened the door and, without any sign of recognition, passed Mrs Post as she dived in.

'I *say*, old boy,' said Willie on his way to the kitchen yet again. He nodded at Mr Osmond's trousers and pressed on, carrying an empty bottle and a nearly empty glass.

Mr Osmond sauntered along the passage, seemed to be bemused by a reproduction of Van Gogh's 'Sunflowers', and hurriedly buttoned up.

'God, what a boring old party!' Mrs Burton said, clutching his arm suddenly, as she lurched towards him. 'How goes it, fellow sufferer?'

As a child he had had a Nannie, who said automatically, a hundred times a day, '*That's* no way to talk.' He thought Mrs Burton might have benefited from her.

'I haven't had a word with Mrs Palfrey yet,' he said, edging away.

Silly old fairy, thought Mrs Burton, who reckoned she knew a thing or two.

To Mrs de Salis's annoyance, Mrs Palfrey and Aunt Bunty were now sitting down, discussing their varicose veins, although Mrs Palfrey seldom went into such personal matters, but Aunt Bunty was so immediately cosy. Their drawn-up chairs spoiled the look of the room, prevented mingling, and made a different party from the one intended. It was not at all smart to sit down, Mrs de Salis thought. She dashed into the kitchen, having remembered some little sausages heating in the oven. In rather a temper, she jabbed cocktail sticks into them, and bore them forth.

Mrs Burton took one and fanned it about before her mouth, having nearly burned her tongue. Mrs Post peered at the dish and said 'How intriguing!' She took the smallest, and gazed at it wonderingly. Mrs Palfrey graciously declined. Mr Osmond looked at his watch. 'Join us, do,' said Aunt Bunty, patting the window-seat beside her. So three were sitting down now.

'We were talking about Brighton,' Mrs Palfrey said, skipping the varicose veins.

'Hove is nice,' he said.

'Hove is *very* nice,' Mrs Palfrey agreed.

Mrs Post suddenly sat down and, holding her empty glass, stared ahead of her, smiling. Willie, coming towards her with the wine bottle, was intercepted by his mother, who shook her head meaningly. 'I think not,' she said between her teeth.

Mrs Burton drifted round the room on her own; she examined photographs, fingered some roses to find out if they were real (they were not), picked up a small china bowl and turned it upside down to look for its mark. Mrs de Salis was glad to see Mr Osmond glancing again at his watch, even more pleased to see Mrs Palfrey, meeting his eyes, very slightly nod. Such delicious complicity, *he* was thinking. Our minds are as one.

Aunt Bunty said, 'You want to be on your way?'

'Want to be on your way?' Willie repeated eagerly, coming towards them. He was fairly fed-up with this whole silly idea of his mother's. 'Taxis are something I *can* do.'

He went off at once.

The ladies fetched their coats and stood about, saying polite things about the party. Mrs de Salis, deciding not to spoil the ship for a hap'orth of tar, smilingly marvelled at their kindness in coming. Mrs Post sat down again. It had all been so wonderful, but she wished that she did not feel so strange and far-away. She was even, she decided, a long way away from herself.

'It's been so nice,' Mr Osmond said once more. The chap might be able to get taxis, but he was the devil of a time doing it. Mrs Post unbuttoned her fur coat. Mrs Burton tapped her long nails against the window-pane – a maddening rhythm. 'Here it is!' she at last said, seeing the taxi draw up below, and Willie bursting out of it.

'So nice,' Mrs Palfrey said. 'Thank you.'

'Really wonderful,' Mrs Post gasped, getting up carefully.

'Have an eye to Mrs Post, will you?' Mrs Palfrey murmured to Mr Osmond. 'The stairs, I mean.'

'Leave it to me,' he said, narrowing his eyes to convey understanding.

'Now you know where to find me,' Mrs de Salis called from the door as they went downstairs.

When Willie returned, she was limp in a chair with her

shoes off, and Aunt Bunty was in the kitchen washing up glasses. The whisky bottle was brought into the open.

'Sorry, sorry, sorry!' Mrs de Salis said, waving her hands. 'Never again, I promise. It was a mistake, I admit. I was only trying to be kind, as is my wont. I did the best I could, as that ghastly old bishop no doubt said to the actress. Oh, sorry, Fay!'

'The little one in beige and grey was drunk, I think,' Aunt Bunty said.

'Well, serve her bloody right.'

'The noisy one most certainly was.'

'She had the gall to pick up that Meissen bowl and look at its bottom.'

'Only it isn't Meissen,' Willie said.

'Don't fight with *me*, boy!'

'Mrs Palfrey scarcely put a drop to her lips,' Aunt Bunty went on.

'Oh, Mrs Palfrey is of solid worth,' Mrs de Salis said scornfully.

'That old chappie is in love with her,' Bunty said, to their complete amazement.

'Oh, how revolting!' cried Mrs de Salis.

'Bunty, you've lived in Brighton for far too long,' said Fay.

'Well, I don't quite know what you mean by that, but . . .'

'Do you know, I believe Aunt B. you're right,' Willie said.

'Don't be ridiculous. I've *lived* there, with them,' Mrs de Salis argued. 'Day after day, I've seen them, listened to them; and I've never heard such fanciful nonsense.'

Willie chewed the last, cold sausage.

'Anyway, I'm fed up with this inquest,' Mrs de Salis said. 'It was a ghastly evening, but I've apologised once.'

Both Aunt Bunty and Fay Sylvester said how much they had enjoyed themselves.

'What are we going to *eat?*' asked Willie.

'Let's go to the Ching-chong,' his mother said, referring to the Pavilion of the Lotus Flower. She felt suddenly lively again, and put on her shoes and got up.

After dinner that evening, the lounge was very quiet. Tourist visitors had departed on what they so often called 'a night on the town'; Mrs Post had faded away to bed; Mrs Burton had followed, angrily, mumbling deridingly to herself as she went up in the lift. 'Gout, that's a good excuse! A bloody nerve.' She had pressed the wrong button and, stepping from the lift, found herself in unknown surroundings. This was the last bloody straw she told herself, aloud. When she reached her bedroom, she was all to pieces. She stormed about, blaming first Willie for his wine, and then her husband for dying. 'You *would?* she sobbed to his memory. 'You bloody would!' An icy little voice at the back of her mind warned her that she was becoming theatrical. She slumped on the side of the bed, and watched her hands swinging limply to and fro between her widespread knees. '*He* would have insisted on me having a proper drink,' she grumbled – her husband now in the second person. After the ghastly wine, she had tried, on her return, to right herself with whisky, had not managed to eat much dinner, had come to bed. 'You could die from it,' she declared, meaning that party.

Mrs Post had lain quietly down and switched off the bed-side lamp. Her head was like a magic-lantern into which slides were thrust noisily, one after the other. Mrs Darling of Peter

Pan, opened and shut her mouth, but nothing came out of it – a pity, for Mrs Post had hoped to remember some of this conversation for her cousin; there had been sausages, she thought, certainly peanuts; Mrs Burton had sung loudly, rather disgracing them, but that was earlier on; Willie had rather disappointed.

'I'm glad I went,' she thought defiantly, 'but I shouldn't like to have to go again tomorrow.'

'Now,' said Mrs Palfrey to Mr Osmond – they were alone in the quiet lounge after dinner. 'There is something towards the taxi.' She had taken a ten-shilling note from her bag, folded it and tucked it under his coffee saucer.

'But I should have liked . . .' he began.

'Well, I like *too*,' she said, smiling but firm.

She is admirable, he thought, dealt with money as a man might . . . no fuss . . . no embarrassment.

'Thank you, then,' he said. 'It was a rum old do, wasn't it?' he ventured. He would have liked, in private, to have torn it all to shreds; but was cautious – rightly, as it turned out. 'I shouldn't wonder if it made one livery,' he said.

'I was fairly careful,' Mrs Palfrey said.

'Well, it was good of her to remember us, I suppose.'

'*Very* good,' Mrs Palfrey said, shutting the door on any gossiping. What an admirable Nannie *she* must have had, he thought.

15

Ludo had disappeared from Mrs Palfrey's life.

'Never lend money to friends, unless you wish to lose them,' her husband had often said. She now fretted about this advice, which seemed to be turning out to be well founded, as so much else of Arthur's wisdom had proved to be. More simply, she seemed to have written a cheque for fifty pounds to rid herself of perhaps the only person she now loved.

Apart from her private grief, she still felt bound to save her public face; although, since Mrs Arbuthnot had left, and she had seen how seldom Mrs Post's cousin, Mr Osmond's sisters came to visit *them*, there was no longer any need to pretend and make excuses. From habit and, also, because talking of Ludo made him feel more real – as lovers discover to the boredom of everybody else – Mrs Palfrey made out a story of increased pressure at the British Museum.

'Is he in Egyptology?' Mr Osmond inquired.

'Archives,' she said, retreating behind that word.

'Must have a chat with him some time,' Mr Osmond said.

'My uncle was a keen Egyptologist. Not my bent; but some of it adhered. I might not disgrace myself in such a conversation.'

Ludo was working in a place remote indeed from the British Museum.

Intent to help his mother and to repay Mrs Palfrey's loan, he had taken another of his little jobs. It was, this time, as a waiter in a small Greek restaurant off the Fulham Road.

The Plaka was in a basement throbbing with *bouzoukia* and smelling of charred lamb. In this deafening noise, Greek refugees became more Greek than ever before in their lives. English Philhellenes *Kalisperassed* about the place continually.

Ludo, always lacking in stamina, found so much exuberance fatiguing. He had to be wary, too. Just when he had decided that he must intervene to break up an argument of threatening dimensions, the protagonists would suddenly smile, throw up their hands, then embrace one another. He had no code of behaviour to go by.

The tips were uncertain: some, as if they were still in rural Greece, left threepence; a few, not yet understanding the currency (and a Greek has to be very new in any country not to get the hang of *that*) left too much. Ludo, loving his tips, longed for some conformity.

Some mornings he set off early and on his way to The Plaka looked in at the art gallery where Rosie, dressed now as an Augustus John gypsy in crushed and trailing velvets, sold catalogues and answered the telephone. The job, although entailing long stretches of boredom, was less irksome than the bustle of the boutiques; the clientele was humble and quiet; tiptoed about, was easily bullied.

Rosie sat at a table just inside the door, usually eating something – apples or pizzas or peanuts – and gave out information when asked or hazarded guesses; but without moving from her chair. She was more offhand than ever. Her nonchalance lowered the temperature.

She was especially offhand with Ludo. He wondered if she was petulant about his working in the evenings, but could hardly believe that anything he did could rouse any such emotion in her. The hours they had spent together in his basement – eating baked beans or lying on the bed – had been marred for him by her indifference. She would languidly be made love to, get up, put herself to rights, hum a little tune, fancy, suddenly, some buttered toast. Or they would fetch a selection from the Chinese Take-Away, which she would eat in silence, finishing with a little sigh at the last grain of rice. Sometimes he would feel, even on the crest of making love, that he was scarcely present.

In the art gallery it was the same. The more she looked at him the more unreal he felt. Whatever he said seemed to glide away from her. People, wandering from picture to picture, lingered; listening to what he said, Ludo knew, listening to his faint-hearted suggestions being rejected. Rosie was always either going to the country to see her parents, or out, in his car, with somebody called Basil.

'Basil *whom*?' Ludo asked sharply, and was at once ashamed of himself.

'Hay-Hardy or somethink,' Rosie said vaguely. (Her mother could not imagine where she had *that* pronunciation from. Rosie, when asked, said she thought it was from her old headmistress: or Sir John Gielgud, or somethink. 'What's it matter?' she would ask, as her mother shuddered.) For they were smart Thames Valley residents, Rosie's parents, and climbing the ladder a little higher every year. Rosie's clothes and cockney twang they tried to be amusing and relaxed about at the Sunday-morning parties.

'Well, Monday, then,' Ludo urged in a low voice. On Mondays the Plaka was closed.

'I happen,' she said, 'to have a job of work to do.'

This was Friday. 'Sunday, then,' he suggested.

He had intended to go to see his mother, then, but that could wait.

His mother, having paid the Putney rent, with Mrs Palfrey's help, had moved into a basement flat round a corner from Harley Street. She was a caretaker for a doctor, so alone there at week-ends. She looked after his Pekineses, as his wife, in Surrey, would not have them. Besides this, she did some type-writing, when need be, and answered the telephone. Like Rosie, she had discovered a little job for an untrained person. Ludo had done the same.

Rosie opened a drawer, took out a long nail-file and began to flash it grimly about her nails.

'Sunday, I'm going to the Zoo with Basil,' she said.

'Well, you can't spend all day long at the Zoo, and that's for sure,' Ludo said in a grumpy voice.

'One thing leads to another.'

This was the trouble.

A man who had been peering at a Matisse print for an unlikely time, glanced over his shoulder at them, and then came to the desk. 'I wonder if you would tell me . . .'

'The price?' Rosie snapped.

Receiving no immediate reply, she pointed with her nail-file at a price-list by the door, then returned her attention to her rasping.

'Aren't you ever coming to see me again?' Ludo asked.

'Well, you work such peculiar hours now,' Rosie complained.

This reminded him that he was nearly due to go and lay up the tables at the Plaka.

'Why don't you come there one evening,' he said hopelessly. 'On me, of course. I'll look after you. It's quite fun.'

'And now you really *have* to be joking,' she said rudely.

Walking along the Fulham Road he thought about love – the appalling inequalities of it. There is always the one who offers the cheek and the one who kisses it. There was Mrs Palfrey doting on *him*, to his embarrassed boredom: and Rosie being doted on by him, to his exasperated sense of loss. But the French saying was not for always true: for instance, his mother had been the one to tilt her cheek, and now was left unkissed.

On Sunday, he went to see her – his dear mother, who seemed to make his feet leaden and put bitterness in his mouth. He walked all the way, and walked again when he arrived, for the Pekineses were ready for the park. Deadly ennui he felt, looking at the late roses, and feeling the Zoo so near to him, and wondering which thing had led to what, in Rosie's day. The little feathery dogs made sharp forays at Alsatians and Boxers.

They walked back – and Harley Street, Wigmore Street and Wimpole Street were like shadowed and sequestered backwaters.

Ludo then typed some of his novel on the doctor's type-writer, and glanced about him occasionally. He saw that his mother had bought a large box of chocolate mints, both *Vogue* and *Harper's*, and was wearing what looked like a new sweater: but he had not the heart to challenge her.

In the evening, he walked home on what he now thought of as his waiter's feet: still more to do before he went to bed. He rolled up his Plaka-smelling shirts and, taking *Madame Bovary* to read, went round to the launderette where he had first met Rosie. This night it was empty. He opened the book, but no printed page could be powerful against his sense of desolation.

16

Old people, those four of them at the Claremont, were early to detect the signs of summer over – a few crisp yellow leaves fallen, some twinges of rheumatism which could now be blamed on dampness in the air, winter clothes brought from the back of the wardrobe, although young girls still went to and from work bare-armed. Mrs Post watched them wistfully, looking out over the spotted laurels in the window-boxes.

One morning, they read in the Deaths column of the *Daily Telegraph* – 'ARBUTHNOT, – On Sept. 10, at The Braemar Nursing Home, Banstead, Middlesex, Elvira Anne, beloved sister of Constance and Dorothy Proctor. Funeral private. No flowers.'

They re-read the notice, Mrs Burton having first drawn their attention to it. There was a shocked silence.

'It seems only yesterday,' Mrs Post said at last, 'that I was waving her good-bye.'

'I would have gone,' said Mr Osmond crossly. 'I should have hired a car.' He glanced at Mrs Palfrey. They might have gone together to pay their last respects, dressed suitably, and in a suitable frame of mind.

'We are not even to know where it is to be,' Mrs Burton complained.

'Or when,' added Mr Osmond. He looked again at the newspaper. In spite of his feeling quite upset, he could not ignore the gratification of seeing in print the name of somebody he knew.

'It would have been nice if we could have sent a wreath,' Mrs Post said. '"From her friends at the Claremont", or something like that.'

Having read the other Deaths, they turned their attention to the Stock Exchange Prices. But a little later, 'I never *did* like the sound of those sisters,' Mr Osmond said furiously.

They could not take their thoughts from poor Mrs Arbuthnot, as she now was to them, as once it had been poor Miss Benson; but *she* had turned out to be a little too awesome for such an epithet. They had read of *her* death, too. 'Good God!' Mrs Burton had shouted out one morning. 'Old Miss Benson, O.B.E., it says. Well, she got that for something, no doubt. Augusta Vivian. Phew! Daughter of the late Helenus Benson. Memorial Service.' They had all got quite excited. Memorial services were like the weddings of their youth and middle years. Now there were no more weddings for them, but the memorial services needed no invitations. 'We'll go together,' Mr Osmond had suggested. 'It is the least that we can do.' 'Oh, what a . . .' Mrs Post began. She had been about to say 'treat'. She slapped her hand over her mouth, her little eyes looking appalled.

But Mrs Arbuthnot's sisters had denied them another

outing. They were piqued about it, feeling, for one thing, that a life and a death were not rounded off without a funeral. Mrs Arbuthnot was left vaguely in an unsatisfactory vacuum. She would be 'poor Mrs Arbuthnot' now for as long as they remembered her.

It was the Masonic Ladies' Night.

Mrs Palfrey came out of the lift at six-thirty, in her evening dress with metallic beads down her sloping breast, her fur cape over her shoulders, and only her rubber-tipped walking stick not 'partyfied'. She wore rather scuffed bronze shoes to match the beads, and a neat crêpe bandage under one thick stocking.

Mr Osmond was waiting for her, looking pink and shiny, and smelling of after-shave lotion. Mrs Post happened to be drifting about, glancing at the menu – or out at the rush-hour traffic. She was a little disturbed. She had known Mr Osmond so much longer than Mrs Palfrey had; and was forced to realise that she had been overlooked for someone of more appeal. She found this puzzling, for she thought Mrs Palfrey – though noble – very mannish in her attitude: that large hand clasping the little evening-bag, for instance, the masculine haircut. Mrs Post had once been thought pretty: Mrs Palfrey could not have been.

The stir in Mrs Post's heart was of jealousy. 'Even if he'd asked me, I'd have been too afraid to go,' she told herself – being alone with him in the taxi, having to meet his friends, wondering what to talk about, having to drink things (Mrs de Salis's party had put her off *that*), not knowing what to expect: it would have worried her to death. But he hadn't asked her.

Summers had found a taxi and, on the other side of the revolving doors, Mr Osmond offered his arm to Mrs Palfrey.

Love of excitement, the longing to participate, suddenly drove all jealousy from Mrs Post's heart. She hastened after them, and waved them good-bye.

Mr Osmond looked out from the cab and raised a hand vaguely. 'I thought for a moment she might have a bag of confetti,' he said, then blushed, unnoticed. 'I mean, I should think she has been a great confetti-thrower in her time.'

Mrs Palfrey said nothing.

'Well, that's a turn-up for the book,' Mrs Burton said, coming up the hotel steps.

'They're going out to a banquet,' Mrs Post said.

'Well, poor old them.'

'Yes, it will probably be quite a bore, I suppose,' Mrs Post said in a sophisticated tone.

'I'll tell you what,' Mrs Burton said. 'My brother-in-law's coming to dinner. I insist – I bloody *insist* – on you joining us. He's not a bad old sport, taken by and large.'

Life was dangerous at the Claremont, and Mrs Post began to tremble.

'See you yonder around seven,' Mrs Burton said, nodding towards the lounge as the lift came down.

Mrs Palfrey and Mr Osmond were placed at the end of one of the prongs of the E-shaped table arrangement. She conversed a little with the man on her right while turtle soup was ladled into their plates – with a little dice of the meat for everyone. She ascertained that he lived in London and spent his holidays on the Costa Brava, and then she turned to Mr Osmond to say what a pleasant change this evening was making for her.

She had noticed earlier while they were drinking sherry that he did not seem to have many friends: the few people whom he introduced to Mrs Palfrey had not the sort of *bon-homie* to match his own; in fact, their eyes almost at once began to range the room for some escape. Rather like a small boy, he had shown off, overdone the familiarity, button-holed men he hardly knew. He was not snubbed; but he was not encouraged. Mrs Palfrey was sorry for him about this and tried to make up for it by giving him her whole attention.

Rolled-up fillets of sole masked with a pinkish sauce followed the soup. The wine, Mr Osmond assured Mrs Palfrey, would not upset her. 'It is quite a far cry from *some* we have been obliged to drink. This is one of the things I know about,' he said, in a tone that implied that there were many others.

Mrs Palfrey's neighbour turned and boomed a few observations at her between courses, while buttering pieces of bread.

Roast duck was served with frozen peas and whirls of duchesse potatoes.

Occasionally, the toast-master would bawl at them that their Worshipful Master and his Lady wished to take wine – with the visitors, or old friends from Potters Bar, or a contingent all the way from Ramsgate.

'I think you must allow there's not much wrong with this,' Mr Osmond said, meaning the claret.

'I'm afraid the Claremont doesn't prepare us for such enormous feasts,' Mrs Palfrey said, striving not to flag.

'What do you make of that?' the man on her right asked her, pointing to the menu. '*Pêches Denise, avec crêpes dentelle.* All Greek to me, I fear.'

'Denise is the name of our hostess,' Mr Osmond said across Mrs Palfrey, who drew back her bust a little as he did so.

They looked at the two figures in the centre of the top table – who appeared remote like Royalty, her pink bouquet placed before her. To have a pudding named after one! Mrs Palfrey marvelled. It was their big evening, those two. They had been rhythmically clapped in (it was rather like a savage rite, Mrs Palfrey had thought), and now presided. She had folded back long white kid gloves off her hands and, from Mrs Palfrey's distance, looked as if her arms were clumsily bandaged.

The pudding in her honour was no more than half a tinned peach sitting on sherry-soaked sponge-cake, and covered with a scoop of ice-cream. From all sides, waitresses came hastening with it.

The Queen; the coffee; Mrs Palfrey declined a *crème de menthe*, which Mr Osmond's late wife had been partial to, he said. She had also liked *petits-fours*, and always said that was the best part of the meal. 'Fish bored her,' Mr Osmond said.

This was really unanswerable, and Mrs Palfrey was glad that the toast-master suddenly banged on the table for the beginning of the speeches. People sat back, expectant, or resigned.

'I mustn't get squiffy,' Mrs Post said, rather surprised at herself for bringing out such a modish-sounding word.

'Now, come!' said Mrs Burton's brother-in-law. 'You're one of us, I know.'

In a draughty place near the door, sat a newcomer, a resident-to-be, if they had known.

Well, if it doesn't suit, it's not the only place in the world, Colonel Mildmay was thinking. He, like some of the others, had had vague ideas about the South Coast, but believed that, as his granddaughter said, London was where it all happened. Bournemouth, perhaps, in the spring. He had sent off for brochures about hotels for retired people, and had become increasingly depressed. 'Standing in secluded grounds.' 'Almost entirely surrounded by trees.' It was no use to anyone of *his* age.

He laid his hands calmly upon the edge of the table, awaiting his sherry trifle, and half closed his eyes at Mrs Burton's coarse, fat laugh, and Mrs Post's new trilling voice.

He would take the porcelain day by day at the Victoria and Albert Museum. Spode. Crown Derby. He would make notes. Here was his trifle – sopping wet, but not with sherry. He suddenly remembered his wife's trifle, and laid down his spoon.

'Not to your liking, sir?' asked the old waitress.

He silently shook his head, as if to say 'Yes', or 'No', or 'No matter'.

Waiting for coffee, he went over in his mind, to hearten himself, the list of inexpensive treats of galleries and museums, auction-rooms, recitals in churches at luncheon-time; but he was not very much heartened by it.

Mrs Post was having a pleasant evening. Mrs Burton's brother-in-law had been at first appalled by the prospect of her company, but soon began to play up very nicely – teasing, and winking, and aligning himself with Mrs Post against his sister-in-law. Mrs Burton seemed not to mind. She made them feel like children as they ate their ice-cream. She lit a cigarette, leaned back, and yawned out smoke, gazing indulgently upon them, with their smiles, and bent heads, and little spoons.

Later, after the speeches, Mrs Palfrey and Mr Osmond sat among the potted palms away from the bar in the Gainsborough Suite. She sipped lemonade, and he a whisky-and-soda. The dining-room had been miraculously cleared for dancing, and they could hear the band, but it was not too loud, they both agreed.

'Mrs Post must have had a lonely evening,' Mr Osmond said. 'We seem to be a long way from the Claremont here: it's an effort to imagine it all going on at this moment, Mrs Post doing her knitting and making for bed.' At the mention of 'bed', Mrs Palfrey quickly stopped a yawn, took a sip of lemonade. 'It's a trivial little world,' Mr Osmond went on. 'Hum-drum. A funny place to end up in. Twenty years ago if I'd been told I should, well . . .' He shrugged, for he could not think *what* he would have said, or done. 'One has a sort of loneliness there,' he said cautiously, 'and a lack of looking forward.'

'Perhaps we are too old for *that*,' said Mrs Palfrey with a smile.

'I am not a callow youth,' Mr Osmond suddenly said. This also was unanswerable and, as no toast-master was there this time to come to her rescue, Mrs Palfrey paused, then took up her glass of lemonade again. 'Delicious,' she said, swirling the ice about. 'So refreshing.'

'But I can promise you devotion,' Mr Osmond said firmly, 'and a pretty fair sort of home.'

Mrs Palfrey was astounded.

'I am asking you to marry me,' Mr Osmond almost shouted. Everything had suddenly gone wrong. His voice was aggressive instead of tender. He was in a muddle, and things meant to be said later had too soon been blurted out. 'Together' (he did not say 'with our pooled resources') 'we could lead some sort of a decent life, be company for one another. Potter about, or go out on the spree.' This last sentence rose almost to a question, imploringly.

Mrs Palfrey said quickly, 'Oh, no, I'm afraid . . .'

He could not allow her to go on. 'A place of our own, a little cottage, perhaps a bit of garden . . . and a nice, homely sort of housekeeper – someone to run round after us on our off-days . . . there's no one at the Claremont to do *that*.'

Mrs Palfrey lifted a hand. 'Mr Osmond, I beseech you: I shall never marry again.'

She was shocked. She had come with him this evening from kindness, for he was not the sort of man that she could ever take to. She had sometimes overheard snatches of stories he was telling to the waiter or Mr Wilkins, the manager, and had been repelled by his eager look. Her husband, Arthur, would have described him as a poor old man, and have set an example of tolerance for his wife to follow.

'I thought the same once, when Hilda died,' Mr Osmond said, suddenly lax and toneless. Then he rose and made off to the bar, returned with more lemonade and more whisky and, perhaps, some hope or courage, for he began at once, 'Just think of some picturesque village – Rottingdean, for instance.'

This was a bad choice, from a bad memory.

'No,' she cried, and her hands flew up to her face like star-tled birds.

'Or Norwich,' he went on, trying to smooth over his mistake. 'I have a couple of friends near Ipswich, who could keep their eyes open for some likely property. It would mean transferring from this Lodge to another, but no matter.'

'Mr Osmond,' Mrs Palfrey began firmly, 'I am honoured, of course; but I am quite taken aback. I had no idea . . .'

'Not of my respect, my admiration?'

'I came this evening as your guest, thinking it simply a friendly invitation . . .'

'Friends we must be,' he declared. 'We are on the other side of passion at our age. Friendship is the lasting thing.'

How did he know – she wondered – who seemed to have none?

As if guessing her thought, he said, 'The two old friends I have in Ipswich, could probably find us something round there for next to nothing. We could entertain in a modest, pleasant way. Small dinner party, the odd cheese-and-wine set-to. I've often read of them, and wondered why we did not think of it in our day. Informal, simple. I have so wished that I could give one of my own.'

So I am to be there so that he can have a cheese-and-wine party, Mrs Palfrey thought tiredly. The band seemed to be getting noisier; the floor in there was bouncing to the thud of feet. She began to long for her narrow bed at the Claremont, and, so, an end to the fantastic, one-sided conversation.

'Well, we have seen what *not* to do in the entertaining line,' Mr Osmond said. 'But a couple of decent wines – a Sancerre, maybe; or a Quincy – do you know that? No, it's not widely appreciated.'

Mrs Palfrey closed her eyes.

He seemed to be talking against disappointment, obstructing her. Filibustering.

'And a red one ... you can leave that to me. And the cheeses – no old Claremont mousetrap or chalky Camembert for *us*. Black Diamond, with a bite in it, a wedge of Brie, half a Stilton if we can run to it.'

All this for a couple of old friends in Ipswich, Mrs Palfrey thought, and wondered if his eccentricity approached madness. He had become obsessed by his imaginary party. Mrs Palfrey put up her hand, from a desire to stem this prattle about cheese. She then remembered her own pleasure of buying the cheese for the lovely evening at Ludo's.

'As I say, we've seen how *not* to entertain,' he said. 'Of course, no names, no pack-drill, not a word even within these four walls.' He glanced about him at the palms. 'I am not cut out to be a widower,' he said in an exhausted voice, 'I have tried it and have failed.'

'It is difficult for all of us to be on our own,' Mrs Palfrey said. 'But that is what I am bound to be.'

'Not *bound*.'

'Bound by my nature. I had one perfect marriage. That suffices.'

'Mine was perfect, too,' he said sulkily.

'Well, then ...'

She was being gentle with him, but he suddenly knew that they would never set up house together.

'Some people are going,' she said, seeing a few women appearing in fur wraps. 'I'm afraid I can't finish my second lemonade.'

'No matter.' He was staring down at the table.

'We shall still be friends.'

'But at the Claremont! At the Claremont!' he protested impatiently.

'It's all been very pleasant, but I think I should like to fetch my cape now.' She stood up with difficulty, feeling tired, so tired.

He was silent in the taxi. They sat looking out of the windows at different sides of the road. Sometimes she made a remark, which he seemed not to hear.

The hall of the Claremont was hushed and dim. It must have been like this for Lady Swayne, returning from her revels long after the others were in bed, thought Mrs Palfrey.

They went up in the lift together, but she got out first. She thanked him for the evening, and set off down the corridor. She heard him closing the lift gates quietly, and then rising higher.

How he would behave to her in the morning was something she was too tired to worry about tonight.

17

The next evening, early, Mrs Palfrey sat down at the desk to write to her daughter. All day, she and Mr Osmond had had little to say to each other, but she had felt his staring at her while she was talking to Mrs Post. Now he was sitting across the room listening to the weather forecast on his old transistor set, which he had turned down low, as radios were not allowed in the public rooms. The light shone through his ear as he bent over the set to listen, shone through his frail hand, too, so that it looked like a web bending his ear forwards.

'I was a guest at a Masonic Ladies' Night,' wrote Mrs Palfrey, proud that, for once, she had something to describe.

Mr Osmond switched off the wireless in his usual spurt of temper. 'This North Country fellow is the giddy limit,' he declared. 'Can't manage to say "Forecast" properly. Might as well be an American. "*Conntinuing.*" Did you hear that? You'd think there'd be a queue of English-speaking people lined up for such a job. Ten minutes a day or so, I suppose. I could do it myself. I should be very glad of a small, part-time occupation such as that.'

He was talking to Mrs Post, who sat near by, playing patience.

He got up and went to the window, watched the evening clouds piling up, and said, 'It seems very warm to me. Unsettled they said, didn't they?'

'I'm sorry. I never listen,' Mrs Post said. 'I always feel there's nothing *I* can do about it, whatever they say.'

'Very true. And they're never right. Here comes the Colonel back from his constitutional. Indefatigable. That's the word for him. Takes the steps well.'

If this game comes out it will mean Brenda will come one afternoon soon and take me for a drive, Mrs Post was thinking, laying out the cards with anticipation – even excitement.

'What's his name?' Mr Osmond asked. 'Colonel Thingummy? I'm blessed if it hasn't gone out of my head for the moment.'

Mrs Post could not remember, either. 'I'm afraid it's escaped me, too,' she said. 'I always have been hopeless at people's names.' But this was not true. It was only lately that she had become so absent-minded and she struggled to cover up her forgetfulness. It was hard work being old. It was like being a baby, in reverse. Every day for an infant means some new little thing learned; every day for the old means some little thing lost. Names slip away, dates mean nothing, sequences become muddled, and faces blurred. Both infancy and age are tiring times.

'Colonel Mildmay,' Mrs Palfrey said to them from her desk, without turning round.

'It was a most pleasant change,' she wrote. 'Each of the women guests received gilt powder-cases as a present. A rather charming idea.' She frowned, and took another sheet of paper, and began the letter again. She would leave out about the powder-case, having suddenly decided to send it to her daughter for Christmas.

The Colonel came in. He was a shy man, who wished to make friends, and offered the evening newspaper about, and said, 'Well, they have chicken fricassee lined up for us tonight.' He had read the menu on his way in, and did not know that the others liked to read it for themselves. Mrs Post nodded, concentrating on her cards. A missing two of spades held up everything else.

'How's your game coming along?' Mr Osmond asked her. She did not know why he was so chatty to her this evening. He usually ignored her and did, in fact, regard her as one of the silliest creatures of her sex.

'Oh, not very well, I'm afraid. I'm afraid I've ...'

'Now don't be tempted to cheat. You'll only be cheating yourself,' he said, shaking a finger at her. He glanced then at Mrs Palfrey's back, but *she* wrote calmly on.

Mrs Burton walked towards them, carrying her first whisky of the evening. She was rather interested in the Colonel; was always *intrigued*, as she herself said, by military men (of rank), and often confessed to have gone about with an American Colonel in the war – 'As every woman in England would have wished to do,' she proudly said. 'And younger ones than me. Bird colonel, to wit.'

'Too what?' Mr Osmond said mischievously.

She smiled and said, they did not know why, 'Boid Coinel.'

'Ciggie?' she asked Colonel Mildmay, holding out her case, and blowing thin streams of smoke down from her nostrils.

It was her brother-in-law's evening for dinner, and she was wearing a sleeveless dress and a burst of diamante near her collar-bone; sagging arms were goose-pimpled. She flopped on to a sofa and put her head back and now the streams of smoke wavered upwards.

'It has dawned on me,' Mr Osmond said, turning from the window, 'that they deliberately seek out those oafs in order to deaden the effects of the Comprehensive Schools.'

The Colonel looked at him inquiringly.

'Oh, you weren't here. The weather forecast, I mean. They choose uneducated people to read them, on purpose. Then if little Willie comes back from his Comprehensive with a Botany Bay accent, parents will say, well, there can't be very much wrong with that, if they talk like it on the wireless.'

He did not see Mrs Palfrey smile.

'You may well be right,' said Colonel Mildmay.

'It's a deliberate policy to foist their educational programme on us.'

'That's very astute of you,' the Colonel said.

He seemed to Mr Osmond to be a very agreeable fellow. He – Mr Osmond – thought of drawing him to one side and asking him if he had heard the one about the man who went into the chemist's shop; but the realisation of Mrs Palfrey's being in the room shamed him. He now remembered lingering outside strip clubs looking at the photographs there, of making, indeed, special journeys to Soho to do that. He shied away from the knowledge of Naturist magazines in a drawer upstairs in his room. These reminders, in the very room where Mrs Palfrey was sitting, seemed to make a monster of him – a being from a different, shoddier world. She could not have understood, and he would not have respected her if she had.

Mrs Burton stubbed out a cigarette vigorously, and the underneath of her old arm shook up and down.

Mrs Post gathered up her cards sadly, and slowly shuffled them. The omens were against her cousin coming for many a long week.

'. . . has asked me to marry him,' Mrs Palfrey was writing. She smiled, with pleasure and mischief, paused, thought she would leave it at that, and stir up things in Scotland a little. She wrote 'loving Mother', and put her letter into the Claremont envelope.

'How did the old prancy-prancy go?' Mrs Burton asked Mr Osmond. 'You know, the dance, the old orgy?'

'I enjoyed it,' he said stiffly. 'I believe we both enjoyed it.'

'It was a very pleasant evening,' Mrs Palfrey said clearly. She stamped her letter, and drew another sheet of paper towards her. 'Dear Ludo,' she wrote, on a sudden thought. 'I should love you to come to dinner one evening. Any time. Yours, Laura Palfrey.'

'P.S. I hope I made it clear to you that the money was a small gift, and not a loan. I'm not sure that, in the haste of the moment, I explained this properly.'

Her letters written, she would have to turn round to face the company. She felt self-conscious and confused, especially as she had had her back so resolutely to them.

Mrs Post laid out her cards once more. 'There's a witch in that clock,' she said, 'holding it back.' She glanced up at the marble chimney-piece. It seemed as if half-past seven would never come.

'Have you relatives in London?' Mrs Burton asked Colonel Mildmay.

'I have a couple of nephews, with their various families.'

'Well, there, how nice. You'll be seeing a lot of them, no doubt.'

'Partly my reason for coming to London,' said the Colonel, 'I must confess.'

'There's nothing like it,' Mrs Burton said cordially, but vaguely.

When at last half-past seven came, Mr Osmond was the last to leave. He picked up the crumpled sheet of writing-paper Mrs Palfrey had thrown into the waste-paper-basket and put it in his pocket. In the ground-floor Gents he smoothed it flat and read it, and was simply puzzled. He wondered why she had not wanted her daughter to know about the gilt powder-compact. He pondered this, sitting at his table, awaiting the lentil soup, and the chicken fricassee.

18

It was a rather beautiful late-autumn afternoon, with a pearly sky, a hint of dusty sunshine. Mrs Palfrey stood with a letter in her hand, looking down at the Cromwell Road. She watched a woman going by, carrying a bunch of Michaelmas daisies that looked webbed and misted over.

She thought of Rottingdean, imagined it, with the leaves coming down – or down already – on the lawns, and this soft-ness in the air; but at the very idea of ever going back there, her heart heeled over in pain.

Although she felt too old to do so, she knew that she must soldier on, as Arthur might have put it, with this new life of her own. She would never again have anyone to turn to for help, to take her arm crossing a road, to comfort her; to listen to any news of hers, good or bad. She was helplessly exposed – to the idiosyncrasies of other old people, the winter coming on, her aches and pains and loneliness, even that absurd and embarrassing proposal of marriage. Rottingdean, and Ludo, too, she determined not to think

ELIZABETH TAYLOR

of – those two happinesses. He had not answered her letter.
She had lost him.

Mr Osmond was reading snatches from his old school magazine to Colonel Mildmay, who had wished to doze. 'I see we
trounced Haileybury.' The Colonel, who had been to
Haileybury, said nothing.

Mrs Post was stealthily taking chocolates from a half-pound
box hidden under a cushion. She would have been pleased to
have handed them round, but once when she had done so, Mr
Osmond had touched both a peppermint cream and a hazel-
nut cluster, before he had changed his mind and taken an
almond whirl.

A photograph of the First Cricket Eleven was now shoved
under the Colonel's nose, so that he might join with Mr
Osmond in deploring the length of the young louts' hair. 'Just
look at that. My God! This one at the back, heh? Old Bordon
would turn in his grave; probably is.' Then Mr Osmond
remembered that Mrs Palfrey's grandson had longish hair, and
feebly added, 'Not so bad, of course, if they keep it clean and
shipshape.'

Antonio came in and removed the coffee cups. When he
had gone, Mrs Post, having pulled the cushion completely
over the box of chocolates, took up her knitting and said, 'He
flustered me.'

'Who?' asked Mr Osmond.

'Antonio.'

'Taking the cups away? They're late with that today.'

'No, correcting my French like that. I don't know what's
come over him. After all, he's no more French than I am.'

Mr Osmond looked puzzled.

'"Abricot", I said. For my little tart, you know. At lunch.'

'Ah!' (As if light dawned.) But he wondered what she was gabbling about.

'"*Cérise?*" he said. "*Non*", I said, "*abricot*", I said. "Oh, abricot", he said, or something like that. Hardly any difference. Just slightly altered the stress. But he knew perfectly well what I meant. In any case, it was apple. *Pomme*, you know. Just the jam on top of it was apricot. I always make a rule of putting the stress on the first syllable – Apricot and abricot. Is that wrong?'

'Not wrong enough for anyone to make an issue of it,' said Mr Osmond with authority. 'Certainly not an Eye-tie.'

In his new mood of remorse, he even felt guilt about Antonio – remembered telling him jokes in simple English, or describing the graffiti of his own country to him. The turned-down expression with which the stories had been received – was it from contempt, or the natural drooping of age and fatigue; or only non-comprehension?

Colonel Mildmay, unable to snooze, decided to go early for his constitutional, and got up quite nimbly from his chair, and quite soon Mrs Palfrey, at the window, saw him go down the steps, and pass along the Cromwell Road, westwards, at an enviable pace.

She should bestir herself, Mrs Palfrey thought. It was not in her nature to stand and stare, to feel melancholy about the past. At that moment, as she decided to go off and post her letter, and had half turned, Mr Osmond appeared beside her at the window.

'You seem a little pensive, a little off-colour,' he said in a low voice. 'Not your usual self today. Aloof from all our idle chatter.'

What an intrusion! thought Mrs Post, knitting more slowly, drawing wool from its cretonne holder, tilting her head back a little, awaiting Mrs Palfrey's reply.

'There is nothing in the least wrong. I was simply watching people go by in this lovely weather. In fact, I'm just about to go out myself – for a little stroll, as far as the Natural History Museum, perhaps.'

Mr Osmond looked at her archly. 'Is that an invitation?' he asked.

The cords tightened down Mrs Palfrey's neck. Her usual consideration for other people's feelings, her disinclination to rebuff him, warred with her fury at his temerity.

In one of Lady Swayne's phrases, she said, 'I'm afraid that it was not.'

They were her last words to him. She hastened, as far as she was able, from the room. She was still hurrying when, in her hat and coat and gloves, she came back across the hall and made a dash for it, as she herself would have described her urgent lope forwards through the swing doors. Going fast, as if pursued, she fell.

'I am Mrs Palfrey's grandson.'

'I rather think not,' said Mr Osmond. 'Perhaps you would care to describe her.'

'No, I really don't think I would.'

'Or cannot?' Mr Osmond raised an eyebrow.

The place was obviously a luxury lunatic asylum, Desmond decided. He had been standing by the deserted reception desk waiting to make inquiries, when this mad old man had come up to him.

'It doesn't matter,' Mr Osmond said. 'Mrs Palfrey is now beyond the reach of interlopers. Mrs Palfrey has been taken from us.'

'You mean she's dead?'

'Mrs Palfrey – your so-called grandmother – has been taken to hospital. This afternoon. We fear a broken hip. We are led to understand a broken hip. A bad thing at our age, I believe.'

Mr Osmond had hung about the vestibule ever since Mrs Palfrey had been carried from it, her eyes closed, though she was not asleep – to the waiting ambulance.

Mr Wilkins, the manager, had been furious at the sight of a stretcher-case being carried down his steps. He was getting a little tired of these old people, with their stingy tipping, no wine at table, hogging the television at peak hours, cluttering up the place and boring everybody. His dream was Conference trade, drinking businessmen, a board in the hall saying 'I.C.I. Pompadour Suite. 11 a.m.' He aspired to that.

'She was unconscious, being carried away,' Mr Osmond told *le vrai* Desmond.

Mrs Palfrey had in fact shut her eyes against suffering pain in public, being carried across the pavement: people pausing to watch, and no Ludo to help her . . . she quickly turned her thoughts from him.

'Where can I inquire about my grandmother?' asked Desmond impatiently; but only Mrs Burton appeared, no receptionist.

'I've told you,' Mr Osmond said. 'We just can't swallow that one. There's no resemblance. None. No resemblance at all; don't you agree with me, Mrs Burton?'

'Who to?'

'To Mrs Palfrey's grandson.'

'*That* gorgeous boy? No, none. Should there be?'

'He's supposed to *be* him. Gives the name.'

Mrs Burton went off into brief peals of laughter, then remembered the sadness of the day. She drifted instead towards a drink.

Artfully, Mr Osmond said to this impostor grandson, 'Well, if you really *are* who you *say* you are, why not get on the telephone to the hospital? Saint Laurence's. You're kin, you say. They should tell you. Miss What's-her-name will get the number for you.' He looked round. 'She should be here any minute. From wherever she is.'

'I'll ring up from home thank you,' Desmond said. And he would have to, he supposed; inform his mother – pass *that* buck, but it seemed to him that the urgency of the visit had diminished.

Mrs Palfrey's letter to her daughter about the proposal of marriage had caused, in Scotland, not just a ripple of surprise and grudging admiration, as Mrs Palfrey had naughtily intended; but consternation. Someone was after Mummy's money and, as Mummy was becoming gaga, Desmond had been instructed to find out exactly what was happening. Feeling, on this occasion, an interested party, he had arrived (but in his own time) at the Claremont. Grannie in hospital suited him admirably. A broken hip must delay nuptials, and he could now, and for the near future go on devoting himself to his writing.

He thanked Mr Osmond for his information and left, and Mr Osmond stared after him and thought how much less callously her real grandson would have reacted. Which was only natural. But a poor actor this one, a most unconvincing – and, for that matter – not very insistent impostor. Strange, Mr Osmond mused.

'Any news?' Mrs Post whispered, touching his sleeve in her agitation.

'Only that Mrs Palfrey will need all the protection we can give her when she returns. Already rogues are impersonating her kin.'

'She may *not* return,' Mrs Post thought – her mind full of memorial services. To see Mrs Palfrey, of all people, being carried down those public steps, in broad daylight, across the common pavement, with people staring (as Mrs Palfrey in her great pain, feeling blood creeping down from her brow again, had realised they would) – that had upset them all. It was like watching a famous statue topple over. Prone, and broken, she was hardly Mrs Palfrey.

Mrs Burton was returning from the hairdresser just as it happened, had hurried up the steps with arms outstretched, had kneeled by Mrs Palfrey and put an elbow round her shoulders, had dabbed gently at blood on her forehead with a lace-trimmed handkerchief. She had protested when Summers and Mr Wilkins came out to carry Mrs Palfrey inside, had said – and was joined in this by Mr Osmond – that it was dangerous to move her until the ambulance arrived; that a rug and a cup of sweet tea would do more good, and to tie her legs together with a scarf.

But Mr Wilkins wanted Mrs Palfrey out of sight. Old ladies falling about. He thought he had had enough. 'She will be comfier in the vestibule,' he said. And, good God! it was bad enough to have her *there*. Someone had telephoned for an

ELIZABETH TAYLOR

ambulance, but they might not see *that* for another half an hour.

'Well, here's a gallimaufry!' said Mr Osmond to Antonio, who spooned *blanquette de veau* on to his plate. He liked the word, and used it for any sort of stew, sometimes ordered stew especially because he felt like saying it.

'*Blanquette de veau*,' Antonio said.

Mr Osmond set his lips together and breathed slowly down his nose, as if this were his way of keeping his patience. Mrs Post was right. Antonio was getting above himself.

The meat was stringy, the sauce gluey. He glanced at the Colonel's table. He was tackling a cutlet, had chosen better.

The place was busy this evening. A couple of men were sitting at Mrs Palfrey's table. The surface had been smoothed. He saw that Mrs Post had laid her knife and fork together on her uneaten stew. They had no appetite this evening. Only the Colonel ate on, as if nothing had happened, and it might be forgiven on grounds of such a short acquaintance.

Mr Osmond's heart felt literally heavy and lowered. Somewhere near his loins it ticked sluggishly away. Why should it bother? Mr Osmond wondered. All his life it had obligingly gone on pulsating; sometimes, of late, in fits and starts. Mr Osmond tried a little more veal then he, too, put his knife and fork together and sat back. Oh, well, he thought, we're all saddled with our hearts. It was a strange old pumping outfit God had thought up on that last day – so Victorian, it seemed.

Mrs Burton with her newly bouffant hair came in late, twinkled her fingers, as if brushing crumbs off them, at

Colonel Mildmay, passing his table. He was eating cheese and biscuits now, and half rose and smiled, his mouth full of cracker.

She's got her eye on him, Mr Osmond thought grimly. It might prove interesting to watch the Colonel's evasive actions. But not very, he decided.

The men at Mrs Palfrey's table were scattering cigarette ash all over the cloth, and Mrs Post, good soul that she was, was glaring at them.

Mr Osmond, sickened by the cold and wrinkled food on his plate, got up and left the room, forfeiting his icecream. He went back to the vestibule and hung about there, as it seemed to him to be the place where news – if any – might arrive: but none did.

19

Ludo waited in the hospital corridor. Other people standing about had bunches of chrysanthemums, and stared before them, as if dazed, at the closed doors of the ward.

Having saved up the fifty pounds he owed to Mrs Palfrey, Ludo had given in his notice at the Plaka Taverna and now was set for resuming – in fact completing – his novel in Harrods Banking Hall.

The walls of the hospital corridor were a chipped dark-green so high up, and then a dingy cream. The smell of antiseptics and of chrysanthemums was ungenial. He was apprehensive.

Bounding eagerly through the swing doors of the Claremont, he had been met with the set face of Mr Osmond, who stood there bracing himself for bad news.

Mrs Post appeared immediately and was joined by Mrs Burton, who described the scene of Mrs Palfrey's fall most vividly to Ludo: how her – Mrs Burton's – handkerchief had been soaked with blood, and how she had tried to dissuade the manager from moving Mrs Palfrey.

Mr Wilkins heard this and came forward in fury. How these old fools hung about the place these days, getting in the way of reception, of luggage being brought in and out.

'The porter and I knew what we were doing,' he told Ludo in a low, but firm voice. 'We are both ex-Army.'

'The Catering Corps,' Mr Osmond murmured to Mrs Post. 'What the devil's that got to do with it?'

'Your mother has been informed,' Mr Wilkins went on. 'It is in her hands now. I am surprised you had not already heard. It occurred yesterday.'

'I was away from home.'

'That will account for it then. I am only sorry that you had to hear of it in this way.' He tilted his head back to indicate the old people grouped behind him. 'Their imaginations get the better of them.' He had lowered his voice even more, and he smiled as if he were talking about naughty children.

The account of Mrs Palfrey's fall had certainly been graphic, and this was why Ludo felt such dread as he stood waiting in the hospital corridor. The scene as Mrs Burton had described it had suddenly reminded him of the old Soviet film *Potemkin* – that sequence of the steps at Odessa; of the old lady, in particular, falling, with blood on her face, her spectacles smashed.

A nurse now opened the double glass doors at the end of the passage, and the little crowd, with Ludo at the back, shuffled forwards, leaving a trail of petals.

Mrs Palfrey was half-way down the ward, her bandaged head turned wearily aside, for she expected no one. When she sensed someone coming towards her and then saw Ludo standing beside her, her face changed, her lips trembled, mumbled in a clumsy way: she turned over the hand which lay on the coverlet, as if it were the only sort of welcome she could manage.

He drew up a chair and sat beside her. Her breathing was difficult, so he talked to her, went softly on, telling her whatever came into his head – about the Plaka, and his mother, gave her messages from her old friends at the Claremont, invented one from the manager. 'They said they would like to visit you,' he said. But Mrs Palfrey, feeling pursued still by Mr Osmond, turned her head on the pillow and whispered, 'Only you.'

'Your daughter? Is she coming?'

'I had a message. She telephoned to say she will come. On the night train on Monday. They have a week-end house-party, for the shooting.'

Ludo nodded, thinking, What a bitch!

'And your grandson? *Le vrai* Desmond?'

'Not yet.'

Running out of things to say, Ludo looked about him.

Opposite Mrs Palfrey, an old lady sat out of bed, in her dressing-gown. Only because of her being in *this* ward, did Ludo know that she was not a man: nearly bald she was, no suggestion of her sex about her, even the dressing-gown was grey and corded. She was playing with some children's bricks on a little table before her, laboriously building them up, then naughtily knocking them down and scrambling them about.

Mrs Palfrey, following Ludo's glance, said, 'I didn't want to die amongst people of that kind. I wanted to be private.'

'You aren't going to die,' Ludo said quickly.

'It doesn't really matter,' Mrs Palfrey said apologetically. 'Perhaps when Elizabeth comes, she'll see to it that I have a room of my own.'

'*I'll* see to it,' Ludo said.

'Oh, I should love it if you could. Monday seems so far away. I should like my own night-gowns, too. And my book of poetry. I lie here trying to remember poems, to take my mind off things; but they're all gone – nearly all gone.'

'Don't talk any more. You'll tire yourself.'

He covered her hand with his, and they sat in silence; she, with her eyes closed, and he staring at the clock above the door and wondering how long before he could get away.

When at last the bell rang, a stir went round the room, people began to give last messages, repeating what they had already said. They patted pillows and made promises, and a general air of relief and jollity prevailed.

Ludo stood up. He put the envelope with the fifty pounds in it into Mrs Palfrey's hand. 'That's yours. Don't lose it. I'll come again.'

He was gone; one of the first out, down the petalled corridor as fast as he could walk, to arrange with someone, if he could, about the private ward before it was too late.

'Pneumonia has set in,' said Mr Osmond, returning from the telephone. He sat down and looked across at Mrs Post. 'That's bad, isn't it?'

Pretending to be a relation of Mrs Palfrey's, he had telephoned the hospital to inquire.

'"As comfortable as could be expected", she said. I asked if the flowers had arrived, but she was unable to confirm that.'

They had each put a few shillings towards sending carnations.

'In fact, she was a little on the abrupt side,' Mr Osmond added. 'Officious.'

'They're hard pushed,' said Mrs Burton. 'I shouldn't want their job.'

'It is a calling, I suppose,' Mrs Post murmured.

'It was moving her like that,' Mr Osmond repeated for the twentieth time. 'I can't get over it. The sheer incompetence! I should have thought even someone from the Catering Corps would have known better than that.'

So knit together were they now in their anxiety that Mrs Post impulsively took a box of Holiday Assortment from under a cushion and handed it round. Mr Osmond chose a Cherry Delight and Mrs Burton took a Rum Truffle. The Colonel declined. He had not cared for Mr Osmond's sneering remark about the Catering Corps. It was a necessary branch of the Service, and entitled to respect. He thought he would go out for a stroll, although he was bored already with the walks about the Cromwell Road; was beginning to think of moving on elsewhere.

'You worked a miracle,' Mrs Palfrey whispered, her eyes roving about the little room where she lay alone.

Ludo put her poetry book on the locker beside her. Mrs Post had made a parcel of some night-gowns and, before putting these in a drawer, Ludo looked at them with interest.

'All out of capital,' Mrs Palfrey said, still looking with content about the room. 'Touching my capital.' She smiled, and winked at Ludo. 'I don't know what Ian will say.'

'Ian?'

'Son-in-law.'

'Oh, yes, I'm with you.'

'I didn't want that money you left here. It was a present. Take it back, won't you?'

'No.' He sounded quite stern.

She closed her eyes, and Ludo got up to walk restlessly about the room. He looked out of the window at traffic and plane trees in the rain. On the chest of drawers twelve pale yellow carnations, curled up, dying, lolled sideways in a chipped vase. Beside them was a card. 'With best wishes for a speedy recovery from your old friends at the Claremont.'

When I'm better, Mrs Palfrey thought – for she no longer believed that she was going to die – when I can get round to it, I shall change my will. He shall have what Desmond would have had, if only he'd taken the trouble to come and see me.

In this, she was for once unjust to Desmond, who had sat by her bed for twenty minutes the previous evening, while she dozed. She had said a word or two to him, but could not now remember the occasion.

Smiling faintly, she let her eyes rest on Ludo, who was bending to examine a chart hanging at the foot of the bed.

'Thank you,' she began. She meant for the room, the visit, the night-gowns, for himself.

'Do you remember the one about the daffodils?' she asked him after a time. 'I can't.'

He knew that she was fretting about forgotten poetry. 'Wordsworth?' he asked.

She nodded. 'I love that one; but it's gone.'

He had been made to learn it at school, and thought it a

dismal, jog-trot jingle. With a few 'tra-las' to fill in what he had forgotten, he stood at the foot of her bed and recited it.

'So much in common.' She sighed contentedly.

She seemed to sleep, and he was just about to creep away when she spoke again. 'Oh, I remember when you were a little boy. You used to hide behind those long red curtains and call "Coo-ee", but before I could look anywhere you'd say, "I'm here, Grannie". You never liked mysteries.'

Then she really slept, and Ludo was able to go home.

Rosie, at a loose end, had called; but nobody was there, and no key had been left underneath the dustbin. She went away, rather piqued that Ludo had not been waiting for her to turn up again.

It was in his own basement room, and not in Harrods Banking Hall that Ludo the next day wrote the last words of *They Weren't Allowed to Die There*.

Having done so, he felt drained of all feeling, and tired, as if he had spewed up a whole world.

When Elizabeth arrived, her mother was already dead. Sister got the brace of grouse, which had been intended to secure favours from whomsoever had the power to give most – Ian's suggestion.

'We found an envelope with money under her pillow. We shall ask you later to sign for it. I can't think how it came to be there.'

'Strange. Was no one with her? When she died, I mean.'

'Her grandson had left a little earlier. She was peacefully asleep when he went. He had been reading poetry to her.'

'Poetry?'

'Her other grandson called once, but I believe she didn't wake,' Sister went on.

'She has – had – no other grandson.'

'Oh, well, perhaps she was wandering, or someone got it wrong. In the end it was a lovely death. She simply slipped away. We were glad and proud to do what we could for her. She had such lovely manners. Always said "thank you", even if she didn't at all like what she got.'

Sister glanced at her watch, and then at papers on her desk. 'Would you like me to organise a cup of tea?' she suggested brightly.

'No, I won't stop.'

(No 'thank you' from *her*, Sister noted.)

'There's rather a lot to be done,' Elizabeth said wearily. 'It's all been a shock.'

Sister nodded and clicked her tongue sympathetically, then took out a pencil and filled in something on a form.

'Tragic, too. She was just about to remarry,' Elizabeth said.

'Oh, how *sweet*,' the Sister said. 'I never stop marvelling at some of these old people. I think, in the end, geriatrics will become my passion.'

At the Claremont, they watched the Deaths column of the *Daily Telegraph*; but no notice of Mrs Palfrey's death appeared. Elizabeth and Ian had decided that there was no one left who would be interested.

TITLES IN SERIES

For a complete list of titles, visit www.nyrb.com.

J.R. ACKERLEY Hindoo Holiday
J.R. ACKERLEY My Dog Tulip
J.R. ACKERLEY My Father and Myself
J.R. ACKERLEY We Think the World of You
HENRY ADAMS The Jeffersonian Transformation
RENATA ADLER Pitch Dark
RENATA ADLER Speedboat
AESCHYLUS Prometheus Bound; translated by Joel Agee
ROBERT AICKMAN Compulsory Games
LEOPOLDO ALAS His Only Son *with* Doña Berta
CÉLESTE ALBARET Monsieur Proust
DANTE ALIGHIERI The Inferno; translated by Ciaran Carson
DANTE ALIGHIERI Purgatorio; translated by D. M. Black
JEAN AMÉRY Charles Bovary, Country Doctor: Portrait of a Simple Man
KINGSLEY AMIS The Alteration
KINGSLEY AMIS Dear Illusion: Collected Stories
KINGSLEY AMIS Ending Up
KINGSLEY AMIS Girl, 20
KINGSLEY AMIS The Green Man
KINGSLEY AMIS Lucky Jim
KINGSLEY AMIS The Old Devils
KINGSLEY AMIS One Fat Englishman
KINGSLEY AMIS Take a Girl Like You
U.R. ANANTHAMURTHY Samskara: A Rite for a Dead Man
IVO ANDRIĆ Omer Pasha Latas
ROBERTO ARLT The Seven Madmen
WILLIAM ATTAWAY Blood on the Forge
W.H. AUDEN (EDITOR) The Living Thoughts of Kierkegaard
W.H. AUDEN W. H. Auden's Book of Light Verse
ERICH AUERBACH Dante: Poet of the Secular World
EVE BABITZ Eve's Hollywood
EVE BABITZ I Used to Be Charming: The Rest of Eve Babitz
EVE BABITZ Slow Days, Fast Company: The World, the Flesh, and L.A.
DOROTHY BAKER Cassandra at the Wedding
DOROTHY BAKER Young Man with a Horn
J.A. BAKER The Peregrine
S. JOSEPHINE BAKER Fighting for Life
HONORÉ DE BALZAC The Human Comedy: Selected Stories
HONORÉ DE BALZAC The Memoirs of Two Young Wives
HONORÉ DE BALZAC The Unknown Masterpiece *and* Gambara
VICKI BAUM Grand Hotel
SYBILLE BEDFORD A Favorite of the Gods *and* A Compass Error
SYBILLE BEDFORD Jigsaw
SYBILLE BEDFORD A Legacy
SYBILLE BEDFORD A Visit to Don Otavio: A Mexican Journey
MAX BEERBOHM The Prince of Minor Writers: The Selected Essays of Max Beerbohm
MAX BEERBOHM Seven Men
STEPHEN BENATAR Wish Her Safe at Home
FRANS G. BENGTSSON The Long Ships
WALTER BENJAMIN The Storyteller Essays
ALEXANDER BERKMAN Prison Memoirs of an Anarchist